SOME GUYS GET

All the Pucks

J.P. STERLING

CONTENTS

Blurb — 1

Dedication — 3

1. Lacey Anton — 4

2. Blake Anton — 12

3. Lacey — 21

4. Blake — 42

5. Lacey — 47

6. Blake — 56

7. Lacey — 63

8. Blake — 70

9. Lacey — 74

10. Blake — 81

11. Lacey 85

12. Blake 90

13. Lacey 94

14. Blake 103

15. Lacey 107

16. Blake 113

17. Lacey 117

18. Blake 127

19. Lacey 135

20. Blake 148

21. Lacey 158

22. Blake 166

23. Lacey 172

24. Blake 188

25. Lacey 196

26. Blake 201

27. Lacey 204

28. Blake 207

29. Lacey 218

30. Blake 226

31. Lacey   232

32. Blake   236

33. Lacey   244

34. Blake   260

35. Lacey   264

36. Blake   271

Epilogue   276

Epilogue   279

Epilogue   283

Bonus Epilogue   286

Bonus Epilogue   291

Acknowledgements   300

Also by J.P. Sterling   302

About J.P. Sterling   304

BLURB

We had the perfect love story...until real life got in the way.

Twenty-five years ago, I won the girl of my dreams, Lacey, but it cost me my best friend, Bill Baker. Now my marriage is crumbling, my daughter is dating Bill's stepson, and Bill Baker seems to be winning at life, all with a suspiciously charming smile.

When Lacey walks out, I suspect Bill has everything to do with it.

I devise a plan to use my sports media company to tear down Bill Baker one final time.

Step one? Send my brilliant daughter to write a hit piece on Bill's AHL team.

Step two? Ignore the fact my daughter fell in love with Bill's stepson.

Step three? Try not to panic when I realize Bill stole every-thing I've fought for my whole life.

Messy, funny, and full of heart. *Some Guys Get All the Pucks* is a small-town sports romance about rediscover-ing the person you fell in love with and realizing some love stories are worth rewriting.

Trigger Warning: Emotional Neglect and Marriage in Trouble.

To the women who never stop fighting for themselves.
The ones who keep going when it would be easier to give up,
who choose hope when the world feels heavy,
and who quietly, bravely build a life they refuse to settle for.
May you always remember: you are worth the fight.

One

Lacey Anton

Since I was eight, I understood my life would be more challenging than most people's because I felt sorry for inanimate objects. Proof: I aligned all my stuffed animals on my bed at night in perfect rotation, so they each got an equal night's opportunity of sleeping next to me. I'd also apologize to the ones who had to lie next to the wall. If they fell off the bed in the middle of the night, I'd give them bandages I made from handkerchiefs. That's not even mentioning how hard my heart shattered for the dolls at Goodwill. I couldn't understand how someone could give their babies away. Don't get me started on my nightly prayers. I prayed for everyone I'd ever met and would often lie awake for hours calling them all by name. If I didn't know their name, I'd send a detailed description of their looks and where I saw them right up to Jesus. I trusted he'd figure out the rest.

Then I blinked, and I'm twenty-five years married today.

And I'm staring at myself in the mirror, marveling at how fast the time went, and just as I predicted, my life felt harder than most. Although, I'd call it my biggest blessing, having four back-to-back babies for the first five years of marriage was the biggest challenge. Add in a career of my own, a workaholic husband who was never home, hockey practices and games for three sons—with my daughter in tow, my plate was full. That was my life for so long, I still can't pass a hockey arena without thinking I need to merge into the turning lane. Autopilot was the default setting, preventing me from noticing that somewhere along the years, I stopped feeling like a wife and started feeling like a really underpaid team manager.

I smooth my hair, debating if I should even bother curling it. Blake won't notice. He hasn't noticed anything about me since the day I walked in on crutches after spraining my ankle while bending under the bed to pick up his misplaced socks.

That was two years ago.

Even then, he hiked an unruly eyebrow and grunted something about, "At least you didn't break it." The sad thing about that moment was his lack of concern didn't surprise me, even though it deeply wounded me.

It still hurts.

I didn't have time to cry. I had to go to work, raise my kids, make the meals, take care of the house. Do all the things. I just kept going.

It's a core memory I can point to as the exact time my marriage took a detrimental nosedive. A line was drawn in our timeline. But twenty-five years together is a big deal. Today feels special, as it should. Not many couples make it this far. I'm putting all my anxieties aside to make sure we have a good day. There's no reason we can't move forward with positive vibes. That's why I took into consideration Blake's strong history of being forgetful, and I left hints about our big day. I literally circled the date on the calendar in his office with a bright red heart. Then last Sunday, I "casually" mentioned our favorite steakhouse was doing an anniversary special—for couples who remembered their anniversaries. When he didn't laugh, I playfully bumped his elbow and said, "That's us, right?"

And just in case that doesn't tip him off about today, I couldn't have been more obvious when I "accidentally" left his unsealed anniversary card lying on my dresser. I'm hoping he got nosey, read it, and realized he needed to do something special for me.

Apparently not.

Blake sleepily shuffles into the bathroom, wearing one of his stretched-out gym T-shirts that he's cut the sleeves off of. Honestly, for almost fifty-years-old, he looks amazing with a toned physique that's only improved over the years. He takes care of his body now the same way he did when he was a professional athlete.

As opposed to me, I've grown frumpy over the years, especially after having so many kids. I eat well, but I have the same foopa any woman my age would have. Perimenopause isn't helping either. I live in a state of exhaustion, and have recently started getting aura migraines that make me forget who I am. In honesty, I need a night out with my handsome husband to feel like he's even attracted to me anymore.

We just don't connect like we used to.

Scratching his belly, he passes behind me without saying good morning and leans over the counter—where I've strategically placed his card this morning—to grab his toothbrush. I wait, counting the seconds until he acknowledges me. After thirty seconds of watching him brush, I give up. "Honey, do you know what today is?" I try to keep it light.

With a full mouth of foam dripping down his chin, he replies, "Uh...Friday?"

I blink, feeling neutral, as I wasn't expecting him to wake up a Romeo. I'm a realist. "Try again."

"Is it garbage day?" His brows bunch together as he appears to be thinking hard before tacking on, "I thought they changed it to Mondays."

And there it is.

The blank expression on his face as he realizes he's messed up, but he doesn't have a clue about what. A younger version of me would cry. It's deeply hurtful to be invisible to a man you spent your life caring for. Today, I'm not surprised or sad. Without knowing it, I had prepared my heart for this let down. I don't feel a sting at all. Instead of tears, I laugh.

He squints at me like he's trying to read my face. "What's so funny?"

"Oh, nothing." I wag my head back and forth as I ponder how to break the news to him. "Just, you know, when you've been married to someone for twenty-five years, you'd think they'd maybe remember you existed."

"Today?" He spits out his toothpaste and peers at me with wide eyes. "Our anniversary is *today*?"

Folding in my lips, I resist the urge to say something snarky. Instead, I aim a pinched-lip smile up at him.

"Oh, I totally knew that. I was messing with you." He forces a laugh, but I can tell he's scrambling. He grabs a hand towel from the rack—the ones I have told him many times are just for decoration—and wipes his mouth and turns back to me. "Don't worry. I got it covered. We'll order pizza tonight, so you don't have to cook. I have a long day at the gym today, and the game is on too. When I get home, we can just eat in the living room, like it's a celebration."

Shocked, my head jolts back.

Pizza and hockey for our silver anniversary?

Why don't you just scream, "I'm clueless!"

But it's so much deeper than that, he remembers the game was on. Even after hearing from me it's our anniversary, he doesn't even ponder if maybe—just maybe—he could skip it to spend time with me. Biting the inside of my cheek, I wait for my heart to squeeze in devastation, but I'm neutral.

I love him dearly.

I always will, but I'm no longer able to be hurt by a man who clearly doesn't even see me. I should be gutted from his neglect, but something else surprising happens. The knot that's been sitting in my gut all week finally loosens. I'd put so much pressure on myself to make this day special—maybe because, deep down, I knew it might be the last straw. "Sure," I say, forcing my voice into an even tone. "That sounds fine."

He grins like he's nailed it. "Don't worry, I'll get the cauliflower crust with vegetables for you." He shoots me a finger gun and winks. "No mushrooms, right?"

Calmness washes over me as I stare at him. It hits me harder than I've ever felt any emotion.

This. Is. It.

Not only am I invisible to him, but he honestly doesn't care about me. All he's worried about is making sure he doesn't miss that game tonight. At this point, I don't think he'll ever care about anything other than hockey and work. The last thing I want to do is sit on the couch and listen to his loud open-mouth chewing as he zones out on the game. He won't even look at me, let alone have any sort of meaningful conversation. I purse my lips out and ponder.

That's when I know the end doesn't always come from a fight or a slammed door. Sometimes it comes in the form of a half-hearted offer for pizza you don't want, from a man who thinks that's "good enough."

And that's when I know.

I'm done showing up for him.

If he wasn't standing in front of me right now, I'd be so inclined to brush my hands together to seal the promise to myself. *I'm done.*

He'll never show up for me the way I need him to. I let out a wistful laugh, and he hikes a brow like he thinks I've finally lost it. But honestly? It feels kind of good. Because if I don't laugh, I might finally remember how to cry, and I'm so over crying about a man who thinks watching hockey on the couch is a good way to appreciate your wife on your anniversary. After a second, he leaks out a forced chuckle. "You're in a silly mood today."

"Yep." I nod big and grandiose. "Silly me."

He turns to leave the bathroom, but I stop him by calling out, "Hey, honey. Are you forgetting something?"

He pats his stomach. "I'll grab a sweatshirt on the way out. I'm running late."

"Not that." I lean forward and pucker my lips. Not because I crave his kiss. Part of me needs to double-check, just to make sure I'm not confused.

"Oh yes." He backsteps, dropping a kiss on the center of my lips, and is already shifting his weight to head back out the door as he calls over his shoulder, "Have a good day."

Watching him walk away, my fingers graze my lips. My heart fully understands that was our last kiss. I never expected to have a last kiss with Blake. Not like this anyway. Not with us both alive, but I know what my heart is telling me. I'm hardly ever wrong.

Two

Blake Anton

Breathing heavy, I rush through the squeaky garage door I promised Lacey I'd oil last week but never got to and enter the house, hours passed dark. Slipping my shoes off by the door, I hang my keys on the black hook. A quick tip of my ear toward the foyer tells me the house is quiet, which I'm slowly getting used to after the last of our four kids just graduated and moved into her own place. With a happy whistle on my lips, I pace forward, but my head jolts back when I see what's neatly sitting next to the bottom step.

Three big rolling suitcases.

"Lacey!" I tip my chin up to call up the stairs.

"Yes, Blake." Her reply comes from behind me.

I whip around, finding her arms crossed and her beautiful chin high. She's wearing a fitted skirt that cuts right below the knee and a matching blazer that's unbuttoned and revealing a tank top underneath. Her blond hair curls in loose waves that hang past her shoulders. The perfume she put on wafts in front of my nose. It's the rose one she saves for special occasions, which makes sense because it's our anniversary. The confusing part is she's dressed to go out, but I brought a pizza home, exactly like I said I would.

And what's with the suitcases?

We don't have any vacations planned. Unless she planned something? But she knew I wanted to watch the game tonight. I can't go anywhere. "Are we going somewhere?"

Her gaze levels with mine, and she doesn't waste a beat. "I'm leaving on a trip."

The words bounce around my skull, echoing. I distinctly remember making plans this morning with her to watch the game. I'm exhausted and just want to relax. Plus, I'm swamped at the gym this week. I hadn't planned to take time off. With a sigh, I mutter, "I appreciate the surprise, but I wish you would have told me you planned a trip. I have meetings all week."

"It's okay." Her voice is calm. "You can keep your meetings. This trip is just for me." After a brief pause her voice grows stronger, and she tacks on, "I'll be honest and say, I wanted today to be special. I can't remember the last time we took time to be a couple. When you didn't seem to care this morning, I planned something special for me."

To be fair, it's not a total surprise. She had been leaving weird hints she wasn't happy with the amount of time we were spending together, or should I say lack of time. It was always in the middle of a heated argument, and I honestly thought she was bluffing.

Because she can't be serious.

She's not going to take a vacation on our anniversary without me.

Her eyes soften in the way I've always loved, but that level of softness is definitely not called for in the middle of a joke. Confusion floods to the front of my brain and I blurt out, "You're leaving on vacation?"

"No, it's not a vacation. It's more like a marriage sabbatical." Her voice is even, as if she's been rehearsing this for a long time.

What even is a marriage sabbatical?

Is she leaving me?

My eyes bug out of my head. *We've been together since high school!* She's honestly the only woman I've ever loved. I can't imagine my life being any other way.

She's my entire world—forever.

That was my vow, and I meant it.

Yesterday, today, and for always.

The weight of her words sinks in, and my stomach plummets to a new low. A sarcastic chuckle bleeps out of my throat, as if I'm reaching for the last shred of this being an absurdity. And because if I don't laugh, I'll crumble. Shaking my head, I reach out for her hip to draw her in close as I say, "You almost had me there. For a second, it sounded like you were leaving *me*."

She steps back, avoiding my touch. Though her steps are silent, my heart hears the echo. It's the clang of her slipping away. "Lacey, you're not serious." I step forward again with both arms extended as my body yearns to connect to hers, like we always hug when I get home. Our pattern is off, and I'm fumbling. Jabbing my thumb into my chest, I go on the defense, "So, this is about me?"

"It's about everything." Her hand flies up like she's confused. "It all built up. It's our anniversary, and you seriously didn't even ask what I wanted. You assumed I would be okay with pizza and hockey, because that's what you want. You never consider what I want. And yes, to top it off, I need a break from your ever-growing trail of socks and your loud open-mouth chewing, but I mostly deeply need some time for me."

"You never told me what you wanted for our anniversary! Why is it my problem to plan it?" I roar as I throw up my hands. "Plus, you've known me since high school. My chewing hasn't changed. It's been like that since we met. You used to love it."

"I'm not sure if I ever *loved* it." She grabs the handle of her suitcase. Time goes into slow motion. I see every finger wrap around that handle, one digit at a time, as if they are counting down the few seconds I have left with my love. I have to reverse what's happening! Then she replies a little breathlessly, "Maybe there's nothing wrong with it, but I need a break from it."

I gape at her as my heart splits in my chest. It's like she took an ax to it. "You can't take a break from a marriage."

Her expression softens into pity, which is the worst expression she's ever given me in all these years. "Honey, if I don't do this, I'm afraid I'll break."

Something in my chest snaps. The single thought that plagued me for all these years.

I've never been good enough.

Even though she chose me all those years ago, her heart was never fully mine. She reserved a piece of it for her first love, my former best friend, Bill Baker.

She'll never admit it.

She doesn't have to, but I can read her like a book. So many times she wore this faraway expression—a sweet wistful smile she never shared with me. Over the years I'd sometimes catch her listening to their song, usually after we'd had a fight. She didn't know I knew that was their song, but Bill was my best friend. He had confided everything in me. My nostrils flare as I hold back the words I can't dare to say.

I'm her forever.

We'd said those vows a year after graduation, and I meant them. Yet, she'd listen to their song in secret, and it always led me to believe she was still remembering him. I did everything I could over the years to win her heart, fully and completely. Apparently, it didn't work. My throat is dry as baked clay when I finally say all I need to say, "Because of Bill, right?"

Her expression flickers, barely, but I see it. She knows exactly what I mean. Her jaw tightens as she steels her shoulders back. "This isn't about Bill. Come on, Blake. That was high school."

"The heck it isn't!" The laugh that bursts out of me is ugly. I hear myself and hate it, but I hate I've had to share my wife's love with Bill more. "It's always been about him."

Throwing her head back, she sighs like she's exhausted. "Blake, you're making things up."

"I know you better than you know yourself." I surprise myself at how calm my voice is. That might have something to do with the fact I've gathered all my stress into the palms of my hands, and I curl my fingers into tight fists that tremble at my sides.

I'd never hurt her.

I won't even raise a hand, but these fists are for someone else. "You don't think I've noticed the way you go quiet when someone says his name on the news or in passing?"

Her lips part, like she's about to protest. Truthfully, I need her to rebut with all the ways I'm wrong. I need her to argue with me and tell me I'm the only person she'll ever love.

She stays silent as her eyelids lower.

And that action is enough.

Enough for my chest to burn.

Enough to confirm every suspicion. "This isn't about him," she says again as she opens her eyes, now filled with tears. "This is about us. And maybe more than me."

I want to yell that it's worse. At least if it's Bill, I'd know who to fight. But if it's about her, I'm helpless. All I've ever wanted to do is make her happy. "I don't understand." My voice breaks. I swallow it down. "I can't give you anymore or love you any harder. If you tell me what to do, I will do it."

Shaking her head, her gaze floats above me as she avoids eye contact, and she rolls her suitcase toward the door.

"Lacey." My voice cracks on her name. I don't doubt my chest is splitting open as my heart crumbles into pieces. I want to grab her arm, force her to look at me, to stay, but my legs won't move. My fists stay locked at my sides. If this is what she wants, then what choice do I have but to let her go?

"I'm going to Mapleton for a few days to stay with my sister, but I'll be in touch." She doesn't look back as she opens the door and passes through. A breeze of fresh air rushes in before she gently shuts the door behind her, but it does nothing to refresh me. I'm fuming hotter than an oven of black coals on fire.

Mapleton?!

Where Bill lives!

Could she be any more obvious?

My body absorbs the lies, and each tremble of my fist fights against it.

She didn't leave me for herself.

She left me because I will never be Bill.

It's funny I don't have any tears, but it might have something to do with the fact that everything's burning. My throat, my lungs, my chest. I stagger into the kitchen on a quest for a glass of water and grip the refrigerator door handle so hard, my arm trembles. I remove my hand from the handle and watch it shake. After a moment, I can't stand to watch any longer, and I curl my fingers back into a fist and drop it to my side.

How long has she been planning this?

How many years did she spend lying next to me, thinking of him?

Had she stayed for the kids, as it's awfully convenient timing with Paisley just graduating. Shaking my head, I can't fathom my whole marriage and the last twenty-five years were a lie. Sure, she may need some time for herself. What mom who just sent her fourth kid out into the world doesn't? But why is she going to Mapleton, the home of her ex?

There's just no way I will ever let Lacey run back to Bill.

Not without a fight.

She's my wife.

I vowed to love her forever.

She took that same vow.

And maybe she didn't understand something about me when we took those vows, but I keep my promises. I will not let Bill scoop her up when she's vulnerable. I retrieve my phone from my blazer pocket, all the while my pulse races as I type a text. Not to her. She isn't going to listen to me now. But to him.

> **We need to talk. There's unfinished business.**

My hand trembles again, and I wrap my fingers around it and squeeze.

Three

LACEY

High School– Senior Year

Two formal dresses are meticulously laid out on my daybed like they alone have the authority to dictate which version of myself I get to be tonight.

The blue one is a soft, baby blue. My mom previously pointed out that hue always brings out my eyes. When she said it, her voice carried this whispering approval that made me feel like wearing it would be the *right* choice. Though it's not exactly reminiscent of a pre-century butter-churning dress, it's one-hundred-percent the *good-girl* dress. It's exactly the kind of dress my long-term boyfriend likes, as he doesn't like to be the center of attention. Always claims to get enough of that on the ice, and he certainly doesn't like it when I wear anything that makes other guys look at me.

It's an okay dress.

As much as I want to love that dress, my gaze drifts to the red dress.

It's not just red, but a rich crimson silk.

I bought it with the money I made from lifeguarding all summer, because my mom refused to buy it. She glared at it, saying, "Red is better suited for you when you're lifeguarding." I actually don't agree with her at all about that. I love the color. I get so much energy when I look at it, and it feels like a celebration color.

Tipping my head to the side, I ponder my decision. Yeah, red is bolder, but when I hold the dress against my body and look in the mirror, I don't hate my reflection. Nothing is falling out, and the important parts are covered. Sure, it's a tad clingier around the hips than the blue one, but I don't necessarily think that's bad. I resent my mom for disapproving because she's the one who gave me these curves. She should be more body positive for my sake.

I press my palm to my stomach, willing the butterflies to calm. This shouldn't be a hard decision at all. After all, the dress isn't life or death. The important thing is I'm going to my senior prom with Bill, and we love each other. We will have an amazing time no matter what I wear. My gaze floats back to the good-girl dress.

It will make both Bill and Mom happy.

So why do my eyes keep floating to the red one?

The doorbell rings.

Bill is here already!

My heart jolts up into my throat, as I hadn't realized it was that late already. I snatch the blue dress off my tautly pulled comforter, carrying it as evidence that I'm almost dressed and hurry down the stairs. Whipping open the door, I lean out on one foot to ready myself to drop a hello kiss on Bill's cheek, and my head jolts back.

It's not Bill!

It's his best friend.

Blake Anton is wearing his letterman jacket and dark jeans, but it's his grin that hits me first. It's smug and maybe even a tad cocky. No, not maybe. Definitely cocky. It's a smile I've seen many times but never aimed at me. He's the guy every girl loves to fawn over, as he might just be the most handsome boy in school. Yes, I have a boyfriend who I love dearly, but I'd be blind if I hadn't noticed how good-looking Blake is.

"Nice dress." His gaze flicks down to the dress clenched in my hands and then back up to level with mine. His grin widens, drawing higher on one side, and my stomach loops.

"Uh, thank you," I say, though my voice wobbles. "I'm getting dressed for the prom. I'm going with Bill." I lean out of the doorframe, half expecting to see Bill hiding around a bush or something, like he sent Blake here first to scout something out as he's planning a surprise for me. It's just like Bill to do that too. "Is Bill with you?" I murmur as confusion floods my brain.

"No, Bill's not with me." Blake shifts his weight away from the porch railing, standing tall now. "But he sent me to pick you up."

My pulse jumps. This is extremely odd behavior for Blake *and* Bill. My eyebrows lower as I toss a quick look behind me to make sure my mom isn't overhearing any of this. When I'm content, I lower my voice, "What is this about, Blake?"

He chuckles a low sound, and it makes something in my stomach tighten. "Bill has a stomachache, and he went to the walk-in clinic, and it's taking a while. He tried to call you, but the line was busy. He didn't want you to miss the grand march. He called me and insisted I take you, and he'll catch up later."

"Uh, that's weird, and doesn't sound like him at all." Bill is the most reliable person I know. He'd never not show up. My throat is dry, and I pause to swallow, but I recall how my sister has been on the phone all night, and likely Bill couldn't get through. "Um, thanks for offering, but I'll wait for Bill." Before I overthink it, I move to shut the door in his face.

Maybe it's rude to end the conversation so abruptly, but my breath is racing in and out, and not in a way that Bill will approve. I drag my feet back upstairs and slip my blue dress on, like the good girl I'm supposed to be. Then I sit on the edge of my bed, waiting for Bill to pick me up.

Which he will do because he said he would.

Because that's who Bill is.

Reliable and loyal.

That's the kind of boyfriend I need.

A little while later, the doorbell rings again. This time I know who it is.

My blue dress flows loose around my hips and hangs almost to the floor. I hike up the skirt a little, so I don't trip on my way to the door. I fling open the door, almost like I'm needing to be rescued from what happened. Sure enough, exactly how I knew he would, Bill stands there, broad-shouldered in his dark suit.

His blue tie matches my dress and is perfectly knotted at the top of his shirt.

His pants are flawlessly pressed.

His hair is combed back neatly in one of those side parts.

He looks exactly like I'd expect him to look for the prom.

He's holding a clear plastic box in his hands. I don't need to look twice to know he has a flower inside. His smile is soft, like he's admiring me. Honestly, he looks perfect.

In a way, it's as if he doesn't know how to be any other way around me but perfect. My chest squeezes. He's handsome and steady in a reliable way that makes sense. "Wow," he says, "You look stunning."

"Thanks." Heat creeps up my neck in a way that never happens with Bill, as I'm usually relaxed around him. Now, I find myself oddly forcing a smile, which is silly.

This is Bill.

My boyfriend, who I love.

He lifts the lid on the box and slides out a corsage of white roses, but that's not all. Nope, Bill is a perfectionist. I already know before I look that he's had the edges of the flowers sprayed baby blue, and there's a matching blue ribbon that holds them all together. He never asked what color my dress was, but that was a Bill thing to assume I'd wear his favorite color.

My throat tightens.

"Sorry about Blake," he starts, "I was at the clinic, and I didn't think I'd make it. I wouldn't force you to do anything to make you uncomfortable. I didn't want you to miss the grand march, but it looks like even if we leave now, it's going to be close. Sorry. Anyway, I got you these." He pushes the flowers forward, and I hold out my wrist. His fingers are so careful and warm as he sets about fastening it. When it's on, his gaze levels back on mine. "You always look so pretty in blue."

My smile wavers. It's a sweet compliment. Something about it doesn't land the way it should. This is prom night; the night we've been talking about for months. I've been dreaming of this moment since I was a little girl. I've got a date with my perfect boyfriend, and I'm wearing his favorite color. It should feel magical.

Instead, my skin prickles.

Not because of Bill's presence, but because of the ghost of another smile that flashes to the front of my brain. Blake's. Curiosity floods my mind, and goosebumps dot my arms.

Bill doesn't notice. He's beaming with a proud smile.

A big, proud, perfect Bill Baker smile.

Then he leans in, his lips brushing mine. It should be sweet, it should make my knees weak, but instead I stiffen and keep my lips pressed closed.

I want to want it.

I want it to feel right, but I pull away, murmuring, "Maybe we shouldn't kiss if you aren't feeling well."

"Oh right." He nods and steps back. "That is a good idea."

"Lacey! Did I hear Bill is here?" My mom's voice carries from the living room. A second later, she rounds the corner with her camera in hand. She's oddly wearing a dress in the middle of the day on a Saturday, which makes me think she's excited for this too. Her eyes shine like she's the one going to prom. "You two look wonderful. Let me get a picture before you go."

Beaming, Bill steps back as he slides his hand over the small of my back. I force a smile, though it feels pasted on. We line up in front of the door, but my mom urges, "Closer." I scoot over as Bill's hand slides all the way around my waist, drawing my body completely flush with his. The flash pops, and my mom lowers her camera. "Got it, and I won't keep you. It looks like you're running a tad late. You kids have fun tonight."

"Thanks." Bill chuckles, squeezing my side. "I know, we already missed the grand march. We need to hurry before we miss the rest."

My voice catches in my throat. The goal: fun.

As we step out into the cool night air, my pulse betrays me. It just doesn't feel like I'm living in this moment as much as I'm going through the motions. The ride to school is hauntingly quiet. Bill drives one-handed with his other arm resting casually on the console between us. I fold my hands in my lap and stare out the window as the streetlights streak by.

What is wrong with me?

This is prom.

This is the SINGLE night girls dream about all through school. Here I am with my best friend, the boy who's always had my back, the one my parents adore. Bill looks perfect in his suit, the faint scent of aftershave wafting off him. *It should be enough.*

But every time I blink, I see Blake's grin.

A shiver works its way down my arms. Bill notices. "Are you cold?" He turns the dial on the heater without waiting for my answer. He's so thoughtful. So very *Bill.*

"I'm fine," I murmur, though my chest tangles in nerves that never used to be there. Or maybe they aren't nerves as much as a sinking feeling. I'm heading down a path I don't really want to go.

Bill pulls into a parking spot right outside the high school. He seems to be one of those lucky guys who always finds front-row parking. As expected, he's the perfect gentleman, helping me out of the car and offering his arm while we walk in. I take slow steps, waiting for the magical goosebumps to come, *but they don't!*

Halting right before we go inside the gym, I stare at him, willing my chest to flutter. Instead, there's this weird warmth that feels more like...friendship. Like I'm standing next to the guy who would help me change my tire, not the boy I can't wait to kiss goodnight. This realization slaps me, and guilt floods in. Blowing out a breath, I shake it off, chalking it up to stress.

It's prom.

Of course, I'm overthinking everything, expecting all the excitement to be magnified, but really, it's just another date. That's all. And it's good because Bill's been my steady since freshman year, the one who knows exactly how I like my coffee—extra hot with foam. This is going to be the best night.

Still, when Bill leans closer, his smile widens like it always does before he kisses me. I glance at his lips, and the bottom of my stomach hollows.

My sneaky brain whispers, *maybe he's just meant to be your friend.*

We'd decided not to kiss each other earlier, but my brain is buzzing so hard with confusion, something in my gut wills me to lean forward. I just know if we kiss, I'll feel the girlfriend goosebumps I need to feel to make this night special. I lean forward, and finally, those goosebumps I've been waiting for all night travel up my arms, but I nearly gulp when they prick little stinging dots that linger too long.

These aren't the good kind of goosebumps!

I squeeze my eyes shut, trying to force the moment into something it isn't. But the harder I try, the louder the truth swims in my head: Somewhere along the way, my boyfriend turned into my...friend. I haven't the faintest idea when it happened, but there's no denying it. I'm getting the ick, and my stomach churns. I place my hand on my middle, knowing it's not whatever stomach virus Bill has. This isn't contagious. This is so much worse. I pull back and smile tightly.

"Look how nice they decorated." Bill's eyes widen as he pivots toward the gym, completely oblivious to my crisis.

In a way, it's the perfect distraction as the gym is alive. Navy blue streamers sag from the rafters, and an off-kilter disco ball scatters light onto the floor. As with every school dance, the music is so loud the floor vibrates with bass. Girls in long dresses stroll past us while boys in tuxes cluster near the snack table, jabbing at each other and laughing.

Bill squeezes my hand as we pass through the wide-open double doors. "Come on," he says, leading the way.

I glance around the gym, and without warning, my gaze catches on a familiar figure near the bleachers.

Blake Anton stands by himself, leaning coolly with one shoulder pressed against the stacked bleachers. He's alone, without a date in sight. His arms cross over his chest, and his dark eyes lock on me like he's been waiting all night. I don't know what it is about his cocky grin, but my stomach loops. My pulse picks up, causing my heart to thump against my ribs. I do everything in my power to avert my gaze, but not before my cheeks heat. Bill's hand brushes mine absently as he leans in to speak above the music. "Let's not waste one moment of this night." He nods toward the couples spinning under the disco ball. "Dance with me."

I let him lead me to the dance floor right as the DJ changes the music into one of my favorite slow songs. Perfect timing. Bill wraps his arm around me. For a moment, everything feels safe enough. But after only a few steps, Bill's hand stiffens at my waist and his smile falters. "Bill?" I whisper. "Is something wrong?"

"I'm fine." His words don't match the wince tugging at the corners of his mouth. He pushes through a few more clumsy steps. Effort is written all over him. His breathing turns shallow, and he shoots me an apologetic half-smile. "Actually, maybe my stomach is bothering me."

I pull back, aiming toward the bleachers while saying, "We can sit—"

"No, this is your favorite song. You have to dance to it at your prom." He squeezes my hand before I can retreat. He takes another step and grimaces harder this time, while sucking back a wheezing breath. His gaze quickly cuts to the exit. Then he scans the room, lifting a hand and calling out, "Hey, Blake!"

My stomach jolts.

Blake's attention shifts in a flash, his eyebrows raising at me.

Bill waves Blake forward and turns back to me, already loosening his hold on my waist. "Confession time: when you refused to go with Blake earlier, he offered to meet up with us here in case I couldn't make it. I'm sorry, but I'm ill. You love this song. Don't waste it because I need a break. You can dance with Blake on this one."

"Bill, it's okay." I grab his shoulder, partly to make him stay. Partly to steady my knees. "It's not about the song as much as it is about you. I'll wait for you."

Shaking his head, he's already stepping toward the exit. "There's no chance I'll be the guy who makes you miss dancing to your favorite song at prom. Seriously, Blake's a good dancer. Just please dance with him." He looks at Blake and says, "Promise me you'll get her home safely."

"Sure," Blake quips, and before I can stop him, Bill's passing me off like it's the most natural thing in the world. I open my mouth to try to protest, but Blake's offering his hand with that cocky smile.

And my heart does an unnerving flip.

I should refuse.

I should insist on sitting out.

But when I raise my gaze to his, my breath catches in my throat. Suddenly, the air around us is different. It's charged with electricity. Before I give myself permission, my fingers slip into his hand against my will. The moment they do, goosebumps ripple up my arms. I suck back a transparent breath. *These are the goosebumps I've been craving.* And for the first time tonight, my heart stumbles. I hate that it's not for Bill. Bill is my boyfriend. My heart should stumble only for him.

The crowd blurs as Blake's other palm slides to my waist. My body tilts toward him like it belongs there. Some magnetic pull tethers us together. It's wrong to feel this magnetism for him. I know it's dishonest. But when he leans down, his breath brushes my ear as he guides me in slow steps, every possible goosebump kisses my spine, waking little dancing butterflies to rip through my gut, planting little seeds of pining I know all too well I shouldn't be having.

I want to run after Bill.

Or at least sit this one out, far away from Blake.

This isn't right.

Instead, I lift my eyes to Blake's and fall into the spiral of sparkles shining back at me. He guides me around the dance floor for a few more steps before the song ends. Then I stumble away from him, completely breathless.

Blake stands still with his cocky grin like he knows exactly what he's done to me.

And Bill?

Frantically, I look to the exit and the bleachers.

He's nowhere.

Blake looks around the room for a second, and his mouth presses into a thin line before he nods toward the exit. "He left already. When we were dancing, I saw him wave from the door and point to the main exit like he was leaving. I could tell something was wrong. He was super pale."

Before he left, I heard him tell Blake to get me home safely, but I thought that was just a weird slip. There's no way he'd ditch me! Not on prom. "I should go," I say quickly as my throat burns with guilt. "I need to check on him. He shouldn't be alone—" But then the opening chords of a new song drift from the speaker, and my head jerks toward the stage. Blake sees it immediately.

"You love this song." A knowing smile tugs at his mouth. "How about one more dance so you can have the prom memories, and then I'll take you to him."

Every logical part of me *screams the screechiest of screams* to leave. There is no point in making prom memories with a boy who isn't mine, but the pull of the song, added to the way Blake's hand doesn't let go of my waist, weakens my resolve. "One more," I whisper.

And then we're moving again, and our steps naturally draw us closer.

Blake dramatically looks down at our feet that never leave alignment. "I've never found a dance partner who doesn't step all over my giant clown feet before. It's like we're made for each other."

A nervous chuckle throbs out of my throat, and my legs stop working as I deadpan on them.

A few nearby couples glance over, but Blake grins like we planned to stop dancing. We're in the middle of the dance floor, but instead of dancing, we're staring at each other, because I'm frozen and can't dance. He doesn't seem to mind though. If anything, he seems amused.

Yet, it's not so awkward.

His hand warms my back, and his thumb brushes absently in rhythm to the music. I'm very aware of how close we are.

If I was sworn to tell the truth, only then would I admit, it feels...*nice.*

Like I could get used to this nice.

When the song ends, another begins, and my feet slowly unfreeze, and I risk dancing. He easily falls into step with me, neither of us saying anything. It's the most comfortable yet exhilarating feeling I've ever had. By the time I glance at the clock again, it hits me. We've danced for too long. I forgot I was supposed to leave. Guilt swarms over me, and I step back too quickly, nearly tripping on the hem of my dress. "I—I should get home."

Blake straightens as concern shadows his facial features. "I'll take you to Bill's house."

"No," I blurt, maybe too fast. There's no chance I'm getting in a car with him. "It's sort of late. I'll just walk home and call him when I get there. If there's anything wrong, I can take my car to see him."

Blake arches a protective brow. "You cannot walk home this late, and in that dress, by yourself."

"It's only five blocks," I insist, fanning myself with my hand. "I need the air, anyway. I'm warm from all this dancing." My voice falters on the last words. I murmur so only I can hear, as if assuring myself, "Probably, and only from the dancing."

His gaze lingers on me, like he doesn't quite believe it. When he slips his hands into his pockets, I know he's not giving up. "Look, I promised Bill I'd get you home safely. I'm not taking no for an answer on this one. If you insist on walking, then I'll walk you home."

My pulse kicks harder at the sound of Bill's name. I glance at the exit, then back at Blake. "You don't have to—"

"I do," he cuts in. "Because I said I would. And because you're not walking home alone." And just like that, the decision is out of my hands. We leave together, the disco ball light fading behind us. My heart hammers for reasons I don't want to diagnose, and the night air does nothing to cool my skin.

Again, it's from dancing.

Maybe from other things I refuse to form into words.

Blake falls into step beside me. I'm grateful his hands are still in his pockets because I don't have to risk craving his touch, but I'm guilty for even thinking about it. "So," he says lightly, "on a scale of one to ten, how bad was my dancing? Be honest. I can take it."

A hesitant laugh drops out of my lips. "You weren't bad at all. I'll give you an eight."

He grins, satisfied. "You're generous. I was hoping for a four.

I politely chuckle as more guilt claws up my throat. I'm supposed to be worrying about Bill. Instead, I'm here, sharing laughs in the moonlight with his best friend. I shake my head as a quiet way to scold myself. "You really shouldn't have agreed to this."

He cocks his head and peers at me. "Agreed to what?"

"To babysit me all night." My voice is light, but there's an edge I can't ignore.

"Babysit?" He gives me a mock glare. "Lacey, you wound me. I'm not babysitting. I'm keeping a promise to my best friend. There's a big difference. Bill felt terrible. I'm just making sure you have a chance to enjoy the prom. Trust me, I know him. I didn't agree to this right away. When he called me earlier, I said no, but he was a mess, and insisted that no matter what happens tonight, he didn't want you to miss out. The only reason I went to that prom was to help him. He really didn't think he'd make it but was giving it his all."

Pressing my lips together, I cringe. This should feel like the swooniest thing ever. What boyfriend is so concerned about his girlfriend's prom, he'd go through all of that to get a backup, but as touched as I am, I can't ignore the fact something feels off with Bill.

My lips protectively seal together, as Blake falls into a quiet rhythm, where we both watch the sidewalk cracks pass us by. I hug my arms, noticing the nip in the air I hadn't before.

Blake frowns, and before I can protest, he slips off his letterman jacket and drapes it over my shoulders. "See," he says, a crooked grin tugging at his lips. "I knew you weren't that warm."

I blink up at him as heat creeps into my cheeks. "I was warm before, but that was before, but thanks for the jacket."

"You're welcome." He shrugs casually. "Don't think I didn't notice you were shivering."

I roll my eyes, trying to shake the tension, but my pulse won't cooperate. His hand brushes my arm as he takes a moment to adjust his coat around me. My chest tightens. A warning bell rings in the back of my head: *Bill is home sick. This is wrong.*

I glance at Blake with his chin set forward, but there's a playful spark in his eyes. It's like he's as aware as I am that something is shifting.

It's the tethering from earlier wrapping around us, drawing us closer. By the time we reach my house, my heels click against the steps as I march up them, determination in every stride. "Bye," I call over my shoulder without looking back. The word is clipped while guilt gnaws at my colon.

"Lacey," Blake's soft voice beckons me.

I freeze mid-step, all the while the alarm rings in my head. *Don't you dare lift an eyelash his way!*

My intestines loop, tugging so tight, I grab at my waist, but slowly, I shift first with my eyes. When that's not enough to see him, I turn at the waist, glancing over my shoulder.

"I need my jacket." His voice's almost shy. "Sorry, I'd let you keep it, but my parents would notice if it was missing."

"Oh, sorry." I slip it off my shoulders and hand it back.

As he receives it, his fingers brush mine, lingering a fraction too long, causing another traitorous spiral of goosebumps to tiptoe up my bare arms. His gaze drops to my arm. Almost like in a trance, he raises a finger, tracing a line across where the goosebumps ripple.

Heat and cold collide, catching me by surprise. My breath hitches. His thumb lingers, and our eyes padlock together. Without thought, without warning, the tethering coils tight, drawing our faces together. Our lips hover for a breath. It's as if all the dancing and all the electricity of the night had been leading to this single, impossible moment.

The WRONG moment.

I'm not this girl.

And I pull back, tearing my gaze from him with an unsteady heartbeat chipping tiny fractions of my heart away one piece at a time. I never imagined breaking up with Bill. I thought our fates were sealed together years ago, but there's no possible way I can pretend any longer that we are okay. If we were okay, I would not be out here on the porch with my lips burning. "Night," I manage finally, my voice trembling. "I—I should go call Bill."

Even though he nods once, I know, somehow, this night isn't over in either of our minds. I'm not sure how this is going to remedy itself. I'm supposed to love Bill, but I'm clearly falling for his best friend.

I tiptoe upstairs, careful not to creak the steps. My mom will ask questions if she sees me now. She'll take one look at me and know something is wrong. Once I pass the safety of my bedroom door, I close it and peel off my dress.

Bill said I looked stunning.

That should be enough because he says and does all the right things. It was so sweet of him to force himself to go to the prom when he knew he was sick. I slip on a night shirt and sink onto my bed as my hand finds my corsage still on my wrist. The petals guide my nose into it, and I inhale the faint perfume of roses and ribbon. It should anchor me to Bill. Instead, the tethering goosebumps ripple up my arms with memories sharp as a blade: Blake's breath at my ear.

My heart thrums in my chest, and I bury my face in my pillow, muffling the sound that escapes me—a frustrated sob.

I'm so insanely lucky to have Bill as my boyfriend.

I should feel the love.

I should feel something else than what I'm feeling.

All I feel is my heart shattering, as if I'm already experiencing a breakup I never thought I'd endure. Deep down, in the part of me I can't admit even to myself, I know tonight was the beginning of the end of an era.

I've outgrown my boyfriend.

It's nothing I ever wanted or saw coming.

Now how do I get the strength to tell him?

Four

Blake

Present Day

It's funny how a house goes from the reliable chaos of four kids and a doting wife to pulsing hollowness. No pucks beating up my basement walls from the boys practicing hockey or music from Paisley's phone. No soft tap of Lacey's heels on the hardwood as she moves from room to room, taking care of everyone. It's only been a few hours since Lacey strode out the front door, and it's the loudest this house has ever been.

My chest squeezes. "Well, I guess that's that," I mutter as I struggle with the urge to be angry.

No, wait, I *am* angry.

I have every right to be furious.

I can already hear the social media explosion: Blake Anton, the jerk who pushed everyone away, until finally, his wife wisely walked out on him. Don't bother with the sad violin. Cue the loser jokes.

Honestly, I don't even care about the gossip that's bound to happen. The thing that guts me the most is Lacey didn't slam the door or throw some big fit. She slipped out the door like it was another errand she had to run. And she did it without a single tear.

The even worse part?

I can't stop wondering who she's running to.

My back molars grind. All I see is Bill Baker's smug smile lit up in a glowing shade of red. He's been up to something. Has he been in touch with her, or worse yet, maybe even encouraged her to leave? It's too bizarre after all these years, and Bill has never married. Sure, he's had girlfriends who the media stalked. I hate to admit I kept tabs on his love life too. Everything always ended too fast, and he's never admitted to any sort of long-term relationship. If I didn't know better, I'd assume he's waiting for Lacey to come back to him.

"Fine," I tell the empty kitchen. "Go crawl back to Bill. You'll see in time that you made a huge mistake." The silence that answers me doesn't sound as convinced as I am. My heart throbs, each blow colors my chest wall a deeper shade of agony: I can't lie to my heart.

I'm not letting her run back to Bill.

If she needs a break, fine. She can take one.

But I will find a way to make this right.

She's my wife, and I will bring her home.

I will never give up on us.

My usual bedtime tapped out two overtimes ago. My muscles scream to stretch out, but my mind won't quit. Hunching over in my overstuffed leather office chair, I study the business spreadsheets open on my computer screen. Sure, I've made a nice living with the two combined incomes of my gym and *Sports Era Magazine*. Add in Lacey's school salary, and we're more than comfortable. Not one member of this large family can say they've ever wanted for anything, but I've also never made the kind of money Bill has earned. That's the truth that burrows under my skin like it's getting ready to hibernate there.

I've spent years telling myself our income disparity didn't mean anything.

Now I'm not so sure.

I think it *matters*.

And I hate it matters.

Tipping my head to the side, my eyes narrow as something bitter coils in my chest. Lacey never cared about wealth, or at least that's what she always said. She acted like my income wasn't something she even noticed, as long as I took care of the bills. But maybe she was being kind? Maybe she didn't want to say out loud that she'd settled. A brick slams into my lungs, and I suck in a breath through my teeth.

I've been comfortable.

That's the word that keeps echoing.

Comfortable while Bill built something massive.

Comfortable while I stayed safe in my investments.

Meanwhile, Bill was building an empire, stacking wins, becoming someone people talk about.

Someone people admire.

Someone my wife might admire.

The jealousy is ugly, and I hate myself for it. I drag a hand down my face, nails scraping over my stubble like I can physically scratch it away. But it won't leave. Twenty-five years later, Bill's success circled back to mock me. A niggle in my head whispers, *This is your fault.* I clench my fists, fingers biting into my palms. Maybe it is? Heat burns in my chest, and something in me snaps inside.

Bill winning ends now!

If he thinks he's taking my wife by flashing money, success, and confidence, he's dead wrong. The mere thought of Lacey looking at him the way she looks at me makes my stomach roll. She may deserve someone better than me, and I'm painfully aware of every way I've fallen short.

But she's mine.

And I can't imagine her laughing with him—or even worse—touching him. That image alone is enough to make my teeth grind. If beating Bill is the only way to keep her, I won't rest until I win. I hate that I'm envious, but I'll use this fury as fire to fuel my comeback.

Five

LACEY

My knuckles pale in the glow of the dashboard as I steer away from my house and watch it shrink in the rearview mirror. The most daunting thing: the porch light flickering with a loose bulb Blake never bothered to fix. I reminded him about it, even though I knew there wasn't a point to asking. Now, it's a beacon warning me, "Keep going forward. He says he loves you, but he'll never make any effort to show up for you."

I've pictured this moment a few times.

If I'm honest, I visualized myself crying. Maybe it's the fact all my babies have already left home that I no longer feel a strong pull from there. It's simply an empty house that's run out of love. When we got married, we were so young, and I thought I knew everything. As each year passed, I learned how untrue that was. But there is one thing I did learn. Over and over again. You can't break a heart that's already shattered.

Heaven knows I've cried enough.

Years of crying over the sink as I scrubbed the dinner dishes the kids and I dirtied from eating alone. Blake couldn't be bothered to make it home for dinner, and the rare occasion he was home at that hour, he'd take his plate into the living room and zone out on the TV. Never once did he notice I was overwhelmed.

Nor did he notice the times I'd sneak out of bed after he fell asleep. My heartache of disconnect was so strong, I couldn't hold it in. Concerned about him, I didn't want to wake him, so I'd go out on the back porch and weep. Even in the dead of Long Island winters, I'd stand out there in my slippers and robe to sob.

I can't say I was ever surprised he never noticed. Sometimes I wonder why I took such care to hide my depression from him. He certainly didn't go out of his way to change his life for me. Half the time he wouldn't even get home until midnight, as he'd stay late at the gym, "spotting his favorite clients." They always came first. He wouldn't even send me a text to let me know he was still alive. Shoot, I'd even cried in bed right next to him while I pressed my head into a pillow so my agony wouldn't bother him.

What was the reasoning behind that?

It's certainly not the advice I give my students. Hide the pain? That's the worst possible thing you can do, and the fastest way to stress out your nervous system. I guess that's why this failure is that much more personal. You know what they say, those who can't do, teach. I guess, those who can't have healthy relationships end up as counselors.

Well, that was then.

Things need to change. From now on, I'll be taking some of my own advice. Leaving the disconnect and constant disappointment to give myself a chance to heal. Since I know there's no way I'll sleep, I drive all night. There's only one place I want to go now. Back home to Mapleton, where I grew up. My parents have long since passed, but after midnight, I pull into the parking lot of my sister's condo. She rents a modest two-bedroom on her schoolteacher's salary. Education runs in our blood, apparently. She's never been married and was happy for the company when I reached out to casually ask if I could visit for a few days.

Everything feels like it's moving in slow motion as I park my car and get out. A neutral expression comes surprisingly easy as I roll my first suitcase up the sidewalk and check for the welcome mat she told me to look for by the door. She apparently hid a key for me. I lift the mat. Nothing. That's funny. She's not one to forget. I glance around like the key might have walked off, and stoop to check under and all around the single planter. There's nothing there either. Tapping my chin, I wonder if I've finally lost my mind and lift the corner of the mat one more time. Surprise! I find it exactly where she said it would be.

Figures.

As annoying as that was, it feels like it's my modus vivendi.

I've been stuck in this state of fight or flight for so long my brain struggles to brain most of the time. The key slides into the lock on the first try, and I exhale, like I was expecting there to be a catch with the lock. So far, so good. I give it an impatient twist, and the door opens with a reluctant click. I exhale again, remembering I went to college and got a whole degree, but here I am stressing about a doorknob.

It's funny how far one can fall.

Without further ado, I grab my suitcase and wheel it inside, parking it just inside the door. After a quick scan of the tiny place, I decide I'll leave it by the door for now. Lori is likely sleeping, as the only light on is the tiny light above the stove. Plus, it wasn't hard for me to roll suitcases out of my home, but something about bringing one farther than the entryway feels a little bit too final for me, like I'm settling in. I'm not ready to say any of this is final.

It's me taking some space before I totally crash out.

My shoulders loosen as I stare at her tiny living room. Just a couch, love seat, and small TV. It's nothing fancy but it feels safer than my own living room, with the largest TV and Blake sitting in the middle of the sectional. That is when he makes it home from the gym.

"Great," I murmur, "I haven't been gone even a full day, and I'm already thinking about him. He's forever on my mind. This is what the experts don't talk about when they talk about leaving: you don't stop loving. Love doesn't switch off like a lamp. It bends under the weight of years until you can't recognize it anymore. I don't have a single doubt that every part of me still loves Blake. I love the boy who made me laugh, who kissed me first on the tailgate of his old truck, who fought for me like he couldn't breathe without me.

Only somewhere along the line, the fighting stopped.

Like a switch, I argue with my own thoughts. That's not true exactly. The fighting never stopped. The fighting for our marriage and for *me stopped.* Then he started fighting with me. I drop onto the couch and press my face into my hands. I whisper the thought I've been swallowing for months. The thought I've never thought out loud.

What if I made the wrong choice to marry Blake?

I mean, it wasn't really right the way we ended up together. I felt guilty about that for so long. What if my real mistake was way back in high school when I got bored dating Bill. He was always a good guy. It wasn't his fault I thought the grass was greener on the other side.

The guilt is instant.

Because even now, with my marriage in pieces and my life scattered in a few rolling suitcases, Blake still has my heart in ways I can't name. He always will. But if we were truly meant to be married, why would it be this hard? The thing is, I meant my vows. Marriage is forever. I don't believe in divorce.

And I don't know what to do with that.

It would be ideal if we could go to counseling together, but he's never been open to that. He's never been open to changing anything, which has left me in this state of exhaustion. I'm just breathing.

Buzz.

A vibration from my jacket pocket pulls my attention, and I sigh. It can't be Blake already. My hand hovers over my phone as I toy with the idea of not even looking, but my mom senses tell me it could be one of the kids.

I pull out my phone and exhale.

> **Peyton: Hey, Mom, I know it's late, but I can't sleep. I was wondering if you are awake. Nothing to worry about.**

I start to type back, but I stop. I'm never up at this hour. How do I explain how I even got his text, but by now his phone has marked I've seen the text, so reluctantly I type back:

> **Yeah, I heard my phone vibrate. What's up?**

Dots appear and disappear and then come up again.

> **Don't get mad. I think I want to quit college. I know I only have one year left, but you're going to find out eventually I failed all my classes this semester. I just didn't go. I just heard from the coach; I can't play next year. I'm sorry.**

My lips part, and I reread his text slowly. Though he's had a nice hockey scholarship, it doesn't give him a full ride. Blake and I have been financing business school for him, as we paid for all of our boys' education. Peyton never once said he was struggling, and as part of the agreement for us to pay for school, we require him to pass his classes. He's always been a good student, as that was also a requirement to play on the team. This isn't like him. My head spins. Of all the days to have this thrown at me, after midnight, I can't think straight. Yet as a professional school counselor, who spends her days talking kids out of dropping out, I have this speech down. My fingers are on autopilot when I text:

> **I'm sorry you had trouble. I wish you had said something sooner. We could have looked at some tutoring or something. I'm not sure it's a good idea to give up just because it was hard. It's**

not good to run away from your problems, as they don't go away that easily. Maybe we can do summer school to
get you back on track. I can talk to your
dad. I'm sure he'll agree it's the best
thing since you're so close to graduation, even if you can't play hockey.
Maybe especially since you can't play
hockey, you will need a degree.

Mom, please don't get offended, but
I don't need your counselor's advice
right now. I just need Mom's advice.
School isn't right for me. At least not
now. Please don't get mad. I have already quit. I'm bad at school but not
hockey. I'm done playing college puck.
I've talked to my agent, and he said
with Dad's connections I have a shot at
the ECHL or AHL. Figured if I didn't go
now, I never would.

"Oh," I say to no one. It's a punctuation I need to allow this finality to sink in. He's worked so hard for three years to earn his degree. It's a shame to give up now. Yet he's a grown adult, who is allowed to make his own decisions. I hate him giving up, but I can't force him to stay, especially if his heart already gave up. I know better than to lecture him, as that will only shut down our communication. I text back:

Well, if that's your final decision, then I respect that, but you'll have to tell your dad. I'm not going to do it for you. And who knows, maybe by the time summer is over, you will change your mind.

I press send, and then quickly send another text:

Love you.

His reply is instant:

I'll call Dad tomorrow. Thanks for not being mad. Love you too. Night.

I drop my phone to my lap and look up, once again seeing the tiny living room that isn't mine. I can't help but think I should take my own advice.

I just ran away from my problems.

What a hypocrite.

Six

BLAKE

(A Week Later)

I don't usually call anyone after nine unless it's an emergency. If Lacey running to Bill's smug face over a week ago, and not calling me once, isn't an emergency, I don't know what is. My hands are shaking when I pick up my phone and dial Paisley, who answers on the second ring. "Dad?"

Music competes with her in the background. It's louder than any song should ever be, which tells me she's alone in her apartment. She's been alone there a lot. I don't worry about her getting her life together. She has always been slower to figure things out, and I don't doubt she will eventually find her way, but when she opted out of college, I admit I was nervous.

Maybe I still am?

She's not as easy as my sons. They are like me. Hockey and more hockey and a nice business school to top it off. I've spent all my time with the boys, especially since they all like to workout at the gym. I rarely spend any time with Paisley that isn't a passing conversation. Now that she started her own photography business and is trying to live on her own, it's been less and less time. It wasn't supposed to be like that. I just don't know how to relate to a moodier version of my wife.

"Yeah, hi, honey," I say, leaning back in my home office chair. "I was thinking about you and how you like to take photos and are good at writing. I have an assignment for *Sports Era Magazine* you'll like, and I'd love to give you the job."

She groans, just as I expected her to do. Again, we don't always see eye-to-eye, and by that, I mean, never. "Dad, you can't be serious, because I hate sports, so I'm not interested—"

"It's not a sport's assignment," I cut in. "It's an investigation. I need someone who isn't afraid to dig a little."

There's a pause, where I imagine her brows pinning together like they always do when she's confused. Eventually, she huffs out, "Dig into what?"

I swivel toward the whiteboard behind my desk. Bill Baker's ugly Granite Ice logo stares back at me. In my rampage, I tore it out of a magazine and taped it to the wall. I circled it in red marker like a target, and it's been my motivation to keep on pushing for the win. Tonight, I glare at it. "Granite Ice." I spit out the words like they taste horrible. "You know Bill Baker, that con who is always running fundraisers to look like Mr. Community Hero? You and I both know there's always dirt if you look close enough."

"Dad..." Her voice is hesitant, like she's testing thin ice. "Are you sure this isn't personal?"

My jaw ticks. I forgot how smart she is. Again, not like her brothers. She's a deep thinker like her mother. I practically growl, "Everything's personal."

"Dad, I mean this in the nicest way, but you have a pretty decent thing going with the magazine. Don't burn it down over a grudge you started as a kid."

I pinch the bridge of my nose. "Look, this is a chance for you to get some professional publishing creds. You want to make a name for yourself? This is it. I'm sending you to Mapleton to interview the players, talk to the families, and find the cracks. There has to be something. If you blow up Bill's empire, I'll be so proud. Not to mention, there'll be a nice reward in it for you. If you know what I mean. Rent for a year." I throw that last part in because not only does it sound good, but I'm guessing I'll be more than likely paying her rent anyway, since she's never actually working when I call her.

"You're so dramatic, Dad." Her sigh is long and loud. "Fine. I'll do it. But if Mom finds out you're sending me to snoop on—"

"Mom won't find out!" I snap.

Another silence. Then softer, she adds, "You really hate him that much, huh?"

I don't answer right away. The truth is, I don't hate Bill Baker. I hate the way his shadow stretches across my life after over two decades. I hate when Lacey walked out that door, the first name I thought of was Bill Baker. I can't stop picturing the two of them together. "Look, this isn't about hating him," I mutter, trying to bluff. "This is about finding the story we both know is there."

She doesn't ask what I mean. Maybe she doesn't want to know. Or maybe she already knows? Did Lacey tell her she was leaving? Who knows what they talk about. I wait in silence for her to reply, because I don't dare ask about her mom. That would be too obvious. "Fine," she says again. "Send me the details. I'll see what I can make happen."

"Perfect. I knew I could count on you. I'll email information on reservations for accommodations in Mapleton," I say. "I'll have everything you need by the morning."

"Bye." She sounds annoyed, but to be fair, she's sounded that way since she was four. She even sounds that way when she's happy. It's just her.

"Thank you—" I start to say, but the line goes dead.

I drop the phone onto the desk and lean back, staring up at that ugly Granite Ice logo. A slow smile tugs on the corners of my lips, and I push the pads of my fingers together, flexing my hand over and over.

She'll do it.

My girl, Paisley, is smart. She'll find all the dirt on Bill, and he'll finally crumble. Then Lacey will see the error of her ways and come running back. We'll have our family back together. As satisfied as I am with this plan, something twists in my gut.

Because if there's one thing I should've learned by now, it's Bill Baker doesn't roll over and take a beating. He fights with everything in him. Which means I've got to prepare to fight even harder. Tearing down his team is phase one of my plan, but it's not going to be enough. I slide my chair forward, grab my mouse, and tap on the Internet search bar. Time to research phase two.

I don't even have Bill's name typed in yet when my phone buzzes.

Peyton: Hey, Dad, I know it's late, but I was hoping you'd be awake.

I grab my phone and quickly reply.

> I am awake. Just working a little. What's up?

> Look, I don't know how to tell you so I'm just going to be blunt. I quit school. You can't talk me out of it. I already told Mom. I'm not asking for permission. It's not for me, but I would like to keep my room at the apartment. I know you said you'd only pay for it if I'm in school. Can I work at the gym until I find a job?

A sharp whistle slips from my lips. That's a lot to take in. I reread it and it sounds like he covered all the bases. He's right. If he's not going to return to school, I'm not paying his part of the rent on the apartment he shares with his two brothers. Pursing my lips, it doesn't take me more than a second to decide working at the gym until he finds a job sounds fair. I'm not going to hash this out with him. He's a smart kid. I text back:

> If that's what you want to do. Gym opens at 5 a.m.

His reply comes right away:

> I'll be there.

Setting my phone aside, I don't think twice about his message. That's his business. As long as he works for his rent, I'm fine with it. I have bigger problems to solve. My gaze slides back to my Google and my fingers fly over the keys: Bill Baker.

Seven

LACEY

I bought a fern yesterday. I guess I'm finally getting used to the idea of settling into Lori's condo. I fell in love with the cheery marigold pot it was living in. I'm not quite sure how I'm supposed to take care of it, but I watered it and placed it in the kitchen window. Maybe I should have read the instructions first before I bought it? I assume it likes direct sunlight.

The irony isn't lost on me that I was upset over the fact I was pouring in a lot of love to someone who didn't show his appreciation. Now that I'm finally away from that, I bought a plant, which is another thing that needs care but doesn't have the ability to love me back.

What is wrong with me?

I've been programmed to care for others over caring for myself. This was supposed to be my time, and I need to enjoy it. Summer will be over before I know it, and I have to go back to work. Although I love my job at the school dearly, being a guidance counselor is incredibly draining, as once again, all I do is care for others. Shaking my head, I stare at the leaves of the plant. It might be my imagination, but they already look like they are starting to wilt.

Clearly, I don't know how to care for a plant. This was a huge waste of money. I could have spent the money on a new haircut instead of buying another dependent. The longer I stare at it, the madder I get for buying it. It's a glaring reminder about my co-dependency issue, I'm only just realizing I've had my entire life. I remember the reason I got married. When I was younger, I used to think the saddest thing that could happen to someone was to end up all alone. That's clearly why I stayed with Bill all through school. He was reliable, and I never doubted he wouldn't be there, even though I never loved him the way I should have. I was so happy when Blake proposed to me. All we talked about was having a big family together, and it sounded perfect. Of course I love my kids, but I no longer think being alone is the saddest thing ever.

The saddest thing is being *with* someone who makes you feel alone.

My head throbs with my almost daily headache. How did I not notice how deeply depressed I was before now? I guess I was too busy to slow down. All my children grew up. Their entire childhoods passed me by while I stayed in silence, suffering in survival mode, and waiting for Blake to magically wake up one day and notice how overwhelmed I was. It's not funny in a ha-ha way, but I disassociated so hard for so many years, I can't even remember half of my life. Rubbing my temples, I take a deep breath. I know one thing: I can't keep putting myself last.

In a need for balance, I turn to my purse that's hung on the back of Lori's wooden kitchen chair, pull out my planner and my favorite pen and attempt to make a list of all the things I can do to create my amazing new life:

- Get new groceries (All healthy stuff. No chocolate).
- Make a list of new clothes I need to buy for work.
- Pick out a new hairstyle and schedule an appointment.
- <u>Don't text Blake.</u>

That last one is underlined for a reason. Then, because it sticks out too much, I add another thing to the list:

·   A small bag of dark chocolate as long as it's organic.

My gaze floats back to the fourth thing on the list. As much as I tell myself I'm not caving in until Blake comes storming in with an apology and plans to do better, part of me still wants to check in. Until he's ready to stop being so stubborn, I know there's no use trying to talk to him. I tried that so many times. It's like talking to a cement wall. He's so lost in his own world, and used to me accepting things as it, he won't hear anything I bring up.

It's been weeks, and we haven't even texted.

Biting my lips, I shake my head as shame rolls in. That's the co-dependency part that knows he's used to me taking care of everything. That man has to be floundering without me to do everything for him. He runs two businesses and has never hired a secretary for either one, because he's always had me in his back pocket, not to mention all the stuff I did to run the home.

He hasn't called yet. He's stubborn, but so am I. If I want him to truly miss me and understand all the ways I was taking care of him, but he wasn't meeting my needs, I need to stay away and let him sit in his own decisions.

Even if I miss him. Even if it's hard.

Call this a midlife crisis, but whatever it is has me asking so many hard questions about life. My throat tightens and I blink, refusing to let the dull sting in behind my eyes spill over. I stay where I am, breathing through it, because leaving doesn't mean I stopped wanting him. It just means I'm choosing myself for once, and if he doesn't learn to choose me back in a way that makes me feel appreciated and loved, I'm not sure I can ever return.

Lori's steps click near the doorway. A second later the doorknob jiggles and she appears, a well-rested smile on her face. We used to have the same smile. Being only a year apart, people said we could pass for twins. My lips pull tight when I don't even recognize that smile. "It's nice out," she says as she slips off her shoes and crosses the room until she's standing next to the table.

"Yeah, I noticed that too." I think back. Did I notice it was nice out? I mean, I walked to the store, but I'm not so sure I even took note of the weather.

Her hand finds the back of the chair nearest mine, but she hasn't pulled it out yet. She looks down at me. "Can I join you?"

"Your place."

By the speed at which she pulls out the chair, I can tell she's stalling, which means she's about to pry. "So," she says as she plops her elbow on the table and leans forward. "How are things?"

I should say fine, but she's my sister. I know that's a waste of a perfectly good word, because she'll see right through it. "I know I've overstayed my welcome."

"Not at all. It's just you said a couple of days. It's been way more than that. Don't you think Blake and the kids miss you?"

"You know my kids." I wave her question away with the flick of my wrist. "They are at that age where they are living their lives, but we text. I mean, I mostly get one word replies from them or at best a funny meme. It's just that age. They are all fine. They don't need me every day like they used to."

One of her eyebrows hikes above the other like it's warning me to what she's about to say, "And Blake..."

Her sentence hangs there, unfinished just like our relationship. It's easy to shrug, but beneath that my fingers worry the edge of the table. "You know Blake. He's busy with work."

"That's not an answer to the question I asked."

"It's the only one I've got." I try to force a smile, but it slips sideways.

"You've been here a while," Lori says again, gentler this time. I'm not sure why she repeated it. It's not like I forgot. "I just...I don't want you hiding out."

"I'm not hiding." A forceful exhale slips out, and then I swallow before I go on, "Okay, maybe a little I'm hiding, but I needed to get away. If I'm bothering you, I can get a hotel."

"You could never bother me," she assures, nudging her knee into mine. "I'm happy to have you stay. I just think we are at that point where maybe we should be honest about the real reason you're here. It's not for a vacation, is it?"

Silence stretches, thinner now.

"What if I don't know why I'm here?" A hot tear burns at the back of my eyelid, but I hold it back with everything I have. I'm not scared to be vulnerable in front of Lori. Aside from Blake, she knows me best, but I'm still scared to admit to myself what's going through my mind.

"If you don't know, then I guess that sort of makes sense," Lori replies. "I didn't mean to make you feel not welcome. You can stay until you figure it out. But don't pretend nobody's worried about you. I am. And I bet Blake is too."

She swallows, eyes shining just enough to give her away. "You always did go for the emotional jugular," I grumble, as I'm not shocked she finally addressed this.

"All in a hard day's work of being your sister." A small laugh slips out of her lips, and she leans back in her chair, smiling that well-rested smile I'm quickly learning to resent.

I could smile like that too.

It used to be easy.

I just need to find a way to get it back.

Eight

Blake

The clang of weights isn't quite as satisfying as the whoosh of the puck hitting the back of the net, but it's a close second. I rack the barbell and, with the edge of my shirt, swipe at the sweat beading down the side of my face when my phone buzzes beside me on the bench. I grab it, and a smile tugs at my lips. "Paisley."

"Dad." She sounds out of breath, like she's been running, which is adorable because she's not any sort of athlete, so I know that's not happening.

"How's it going?" Loading another plate on the bar, I pretend my question is casual when really my gut is looping into knots. I haven't heard from her since she arrived in Mapleton to spy on Bill's team, and I'm dying to hear all the tea.

"Fine, well, good, actually. Bill's been oddly welcoming. He even offered me an office space in his arena. Like, I'm seriously right down the hall from him. Nobody is paying attention to what I do or where I go. I have so much access to all these guys, and I can hear all their conversations."

"That's interesting." Despite her enthusiasm, my jaw clenches. Bill is by all definitions of the word a "nice guy," but I don't doubt he's using her for his own agenda. Now I just have to find out what that agenda is. He's more than likely keeping her there so he can keep tabs on her.

"The bad news isssss," she draws out the word like she knows I'm about to overreact. "I might've lost the magazine camera, but it's handled. I'm working with one of the players to get some shots sent to me to replace the coverage I lost. It's actually turning out well, because they trust him. The result is everyone is sending me all sorts of personal photos."

I nearly drop the plate. I couldn't care less about the camera at this point. I don't like the sound of the other thing she said. "Wait? Who? Which player is helping you?"

"Dad, relax. It's nothing to be concerned about. He's being nice."

"Nice is how it starts." Panic floods into my chest. This is the last thing I need. Paisley is usually shy and at the very least not approachable. I never expected her to get close to any of the guys, or I would have never sent her. "Next thing you know, he's asking you out," I spit out as my thoughts won't stay silent. "What is his name?"

She laughs. "You're paranoid."

"What's his name, Paisley?" Gritting my teeth, I pace the length of the squat rack, my pulse spiking faster than it did under the weights.

"Noah Miller."

I purse my lips. It doesn't ring a bell, but I still don't trust him. "Just don't get cozy with him—or anyone. You're there to work. The last thing you need to do is make friends, or worse yet, get some stupid crush on one of these guys. Remember, they are the enemy. Don't forget that."

"Fine, fine," she says, clearly humoring me. Then, before I can press further, she changes the subject. "So, is Mom around. Can I talk to her?"

The question slams against my chest. I grip the phone tighter as my throat cinches. I'm assuming Paisley doesn't know that we're on a marriage sabbatical. None of the kids actually know anything, as far as I'm aware. I'm still holding out hope we can fix us. I'm not going to tell them before they find out. "No, I'm at the gym right now, but she's at home, and she's good," I lie.

There's a pause, like she's not sure she believes me. Then she sighs. "Okay. Well, I'll keep you posted about anything I find out."

"Do that." My voice comes out rougher than I want. I hate how hard life is right now. I'm supposed to be enjoying this stage of my life as an empty nester with my beautiful wife. Instead of booking weekend trips for just us, we're falling apart.

Paisley hangs up first, and I stand with the phone in my hand, feeling the weight of everything pressing down on me. I hate it. So, I rack another plate on the bar, loading on more weight than I lifted in years. If I can't hold my family together, the least I can do is hold this.

And maybe, if I get strong enough, it won't hurt as much if it falls apart for good.

Too bad they don't make barbells for my heart.

Nine

Lacey

Not to be dramatic, but actually yes, to be dramatic, it was all claustrophobia's fault. It wrapped around me in the condo so tightly, I thought I was going to suffocate. So, I went for a walk. I knew better than to walk to the grocery store because I'd likely come out of it with a giant bag of chocolate my hips don't need and another plant I have to take care of. I steered in the other direction and quickly got sucked into the nostalgia of my youth when I ended up at the park, drawn by muscle memory more than logic.

I should have known better.

Because Bill Baker is standing right next to the ice rink in a Granite Ice polo, and it looks like his team's doing some meet-and-greet with town members. Just like that, two decades evaporate in a blink. His hair is gray at the temples now, but his jawline is still snatched. If I blur my vision a little, it doesn't look like a day has passed.

My stomach twists, warning me to turn around.

It's best not to open that door. I don't need a reunion with him, I don't pine for him, and I need to work things out with my husband. Rehashing old memories with Bill will only make things worse. Pretending not to see him, I slide my foot backward.

Unlucky for me, he spots me!

In my peripheral vision, I clearly see his jaw drop, and a beat later, he calls out, "Lacey?" His voice pings exactly the same, an echo of my seventeen-year-old self in my chest.

Oh man, I'm cooked.

I freeze as I wait for him to cross the park with an impossible to miss smile tugging at his mouth. "Hi, Bill." I manage to throw up my hand in a wave. He's close enough now that I can see the flicker in his eyes, like he's remembering too.

Before he can say anything, a woman steps out from a food truck line. Without noticing me, she calls out, "Bill, they had two burgers left, so I grabbed them both."

My breath hitches in the back of my throat. I'm sure it looks like I'm staring, but for the life of me I can't stop. She's younger than me. Maybe. Her hair pulled into a ponytail. By every measure, she's radiant. Bill's smile stretches wider as she approaches. There's pride written all over his face. He takes her hand into his and then turns back to me. "Lacey," he shifts his weight from one leg to the other. "Meet my wife, Ruth."

Wife.

The word thumps into my chest. I smile automatically, because that's what polite people do. To avoid making this anymore awkward, I hold out my hand until she takes it, and we shake, and I cheerfully say, "It's nice to meet you, Ruth."

Ruth beams. I wouldn't believe it if I wasn't standing right here, but she grows even prettier as her eyes sparkle back. "You too. I've heard your name before. Bill told me all about his old high school days."

My chest squeezes tighter.

His old high school days?

Or is it our old high school days?

I'm not sure why this affects me the way it does. I'm completely unprepared for this conversation. I cut my gaze back at Bill, who's looking at me, but not in the way Blake does. Bill's attention is friendly, as if he's genuinely glad to run into me, but I'm not his favorite person on the planet. It's crazy how this feels after all these years. I wasn't exactly expecting him to hold a grudge against me for breaking his heart all those years ago, but it's almost like I was never special at all.

I get it.

Bill's built a life.

Just as I did.

I never pined for him in any way, and I'm happy to see him finally get his happy ever after. He certainly waited long enough. I tuck my hair behind my ear. "Well, congratulations on your marriage. You both look happy."

It's the truth. She's glowing, and he's gleaming back at her.

So not how Blake and my relationship turned out at all.

"Thanks," Bill says softly as he stares back at her, like he can't bear to take his attention off his beautiful love. He barely looks at me when he says, "Really good to see you, Lacey."

I nod, stepping back, suddenly desperate for air. "You too." I stride away as fast as I can, shaking my head the whole time. How stupid was I for even going there. I'm not in Long Island anymore. This is Mapleton, Bill's stomping grounds. Yes, it used to be mine, but he's clearly the golden boy here. By the time I make it around the corner, my chest is heaving. I press a hand to my heart, willing it to steady. Bill's moved on with a lovely lady, who I don't doubt makes him happy from the expression on his face. I don't even care about Bill, but somehow seeing him so happy makes me see my truth so much clearer. I moved on, but I'm not happy.

Not like that.

I storm four blocks back to the apartment while my brain fogs with all the things that have been bothering me over the years. I get that I can't change anyone. I can only change myself. That's what I'm trying to do by working on myself, but it's hard not to wonder if maybe I'd made a mistake when I rushed to marry so fast after high school. We were just babies.

I unlock the apartment door and kick off my shoes, pushing them against the wall and out of the way, since this apartment is too tiny to even have an entryway closet. It's a big change from my three-thousand-foot home with an entire walk-in mud room closet. I cross the living room in four steps, plopping onto the couch, while my heart stays in my throat, cinching so tightly.

They say comparison is the thief of joy. I'm not trying to compare my life to anyone, but I have to ask the question: what am I doing here with suitcases that aren't fully unpacked after weeks because unpacking feels too final?

My chest aches with shame.

How selfish that a part of me thought I could leave Blake and rewrite my life like the last twenty years didn't matter, and it's not going to impact me. Did I seriously think coming here would flip a switch in my brain, and I'd be so blissfully happy just from the change of scenery? I press my palms to my eyes until colors spark. Because the truth is clearer than it ever has been, the grass isn't any greener here. It's actually just as lonely, if not more. Blake was a risk I took two decades ago, but he took a risk on me too.

And I loved him for it.

For many years I thought he'd saved me from a boring life with Bill. I don't think I'd ever broken up with Bill if Blake hadn't come along. Bill was safe and everyone loved him, especially my parents. But seeing Bill tonight makes me understand on a deeper level that we both had our own paths, and they were never together.

I didn't make a mistake.

I followed my heart to Blake because I loved him.

I still do.

The thought slices through me like glass. I curl forward, clutching my knees, breathing hard. I don't doubt I love Blake, but why can't I be happy? The hurt inside of me runs deeper than just my issues with Blake. Maybe I covered it up all those years because I was too busy surviving four kids to feel it? My head starts to pound with my all-too common-these-days-stress headache. This is about wanting to find the girl I lost somewhere along the way. The one who laughed too loud, dreamed big, and believed she deserved more than silence when her husband sat across from her on the couch to eat dinner. Like seriously, I deserve a husband who will at least sit at the table with me. I know I can't change him, but I'm hoping some time apart will help him appreciate me.

If this doesn't work, I don't know what else to do.

I just want to be happy again, and I want Blake to want that for me too. If he would only notice.

Ten

BLAKE

With only the sporadic rattle of weights from my two late-night regulars, my gym remains quiet. Not as quiet as my house though. That's why I insisted these guys were welcome to stay late. I certainly don't need to go home to an empty house. Going to bed is pointless too, as I haven't been sleeping. I'm either lying in bed all night, counting the dots on the popcorn-textured ceiling, replaying every single moment I can think of to question my self-worth, or I scroll hockey reels while also keeping the game on the bedroom TV, so there isn't a moment of accidental silence because the last thing I want to do is face the reality that my Lacey is gone.

Sometimes my methods work.

More often I tell myself they work when they are actually worthless.

I have learned one important thing since Lacey left.

Home isn't home without Lacey.

So, even though my arms are shaking from already doubling my normal workout, I lie back on the bench, grind out another set, and another after that. My muscles scream, but it's the kind of pain I welcome. Nothing dulls my thoughts completely, but it helps to distract me from the heartbreak I can't numb. When my phone buzzes, I'm frantic to see who it is, even though my heart already knows it's not Lacey.

Paisley.

I wipe my hands on a towel and tuck my phone between my ear and shoulder. "Yeah?"

"Dad." Her voice is upbeat for once. "I want to let you know the camera was returned. I'm not sure who found it. It was in my office with no note, but unfortunately, it's broken." Then she rushes out the next part, "I'm going to use my money to fix it."

"That's good and bad, I guess." I chuckle with the mixed news. "Maybe use it as a lesson to keep better track of it. I don't think you need to pay for it though. It belongs to the magazine. We can expense the repairs this one time if you promise to be more careful."

"I will." She sighs, like she's relieved I didn't give her the full lecture. Then her voice brightens again. "Anyway, things are going surprisingly well here. They have one player, Axl, who has the cockiest mouth I've ever heard. He loves getting into fights. I'm sure it won't be long, and he'll give me a story to make them look bad. And Bill's stepson has been helping me—"

Ice floods through my veins at lightning speed, and I cut her off, "His *stepson?*"

"Yeah," she says, casual as anything. "Noah, the one I told you about before. He's on the team. He's actually a pretty fast skater. All the fans are crazy about him, and he's been helping—"

The words hit me like a puck to the ribs.

Stepson.

Bill Baker is married.

All these years, I've carried this grudge like a scar as I was convinced he lurked in the shadows, waiting to swoop in and take back what he thought was his. I was fully convinced Lacey never stopped loving him, and if she'd get the chance, she'd go running right back.

And he's been married!

"Dad?" Her voice breaks my thoughts. "Are you still there?"

I clear my throat. "Yeah. Sorry, I was helping a client."

"You sound distracted by something."

"No." I grip the phone tighter. She doesn't need to know about my confliction. She needs to think this is only about an old hockey rivalry. I swallow hard as my gut twists. If Bill's married, Lacey isn't running back to him, but pride is stubborn. Part of me still believes Lacey would return to him if the chance was there. It's too soon to call off the investigation. "Well, honey, I'm glad you got the camera back," I say to fill in the silence before Paisley gets suspicious about my motives again. "I can't wait to read your article. It will be amazing."

"Yeah, you won't be disappointed." Her voice is a tad uneven, and she's fast to hang up after blurting out. "But, anyway, I have to go. Talk to you later." I stare at her name blinking on my screen when a new thought pops in my head. If Bill is married, is he even my problem anymore?

Or maybe he never really was.

Maybe there's something else I need to worry about?

Could the failure of my marriage possibly be my fault?

I dig deep in my brain, thinking of something I may have done to make Lacey leave me, but there's nothing. Shaking my head, I mutter, "Nah, I'm a great husband. What could possibly be wrong with me?"

Eleven

LACEY

The days go by in a haze of everyday moments. Grocery store. A random walk where I avoid the park. Dinner that doesn't include chocolate. Headaches. Snacks that include chocolate. Watering my plant. Napping. Texting the kids. More chocolate. Making up excuses to why I'm not at the house when a kid randomly drops by to say hi. Avoiding Blake's texts. Overthinking every single decision I've made in the last three decades. More headaches. More chocolate. Then it is over, and I pack my car and say goodbye to Mapleton, not any clearer about what I want.

I know I'm NOT ready to go back to the house, so I book an Airbnb. It's pricey and takes a good chunk of my modest income. At least for right now, I want a smooth transition back into school. It's crazy how I could be gone so long and still not feel...right.

My nervous system isn't as calm as I would have thought it would be. I'm still getting migraines, and my heart is in scattered fragments. The professional advice I'd give myself is the body eventually cries out with all the words you've silenced. The book smart part of my brain understands completely why I'm so burned out, but that doesn't make it any easier to heal.

Nonetheless, time doesn't stay still for me. It's the first week of school, which always feels like a marathon in heels. The funny thing is, I've long since ditched the heels and invested in orthotics. Spoiler alert: my feet still ache. By the time Friday hits, my desk looks like a hurricane swept through it with piles of forms and multicolored sticky notes plastered everywhere. Yet, despite the chaos, I love my job. I've been the head school counselor since my kids started going to school here. As much as I get overwhelmed, it fills me with hope to see the students return each year. I sigh as I plop down on my chair to answer the never-ending list of emails I still need to follow up on.

"Mrs. Anton?" A timid knock on the door pulls me from my computer screen. "Do you have a minute?"

A new student I've yet to meet hovers in front of me with puffy eyes, and she's clasping her phone in front of her. So much for answering emails.

"Of course." I gesture to the armchair across from me and glance at the clock. I was really hoping to be done with my workday. The final bell's about to ring, but one more student won't hold me up too long. At least I hope that's not me having wishful thinking here. I pinch back the sigh begging to come out. "Come in. Sit down. Tell me your name and what's going on." Adjusting myself for a long sit, I sink into the backrest on my desk chair, grateful it's so comfortable.

"Bailey Morgan." She barely gets the words out, and tears slip down her cheeks. I grab the tissues on my desk and offer the whole box to her. It's an automatic response I don't even have to think about as students crying in my office is a daily thing.

Two minutes of high-pitched static. That's what her voice feels like—a high-pitch cry about how Mr. Roads "literally has a vendetta against her because she's a cheerleader" after four days of algebra, and how her mother's demand for passing grades is "impossible." She threatens running away while her hands fly in a frantic blur of expensively manicured acrylic nails, which I don't doubt her "mean mom" pays for.

I keep my nodding rhythmic. "The first week is always the hardest." My voice drops into a grounding register I've perfected. I don't tell her that her life is a cakewalk. I remember being her age and being so stressed over every little decision. What she doesn't see is that her decisions aren't life threatening. Most of the things she's living through right now will be gone in a few months. Still, I do my best to help her by giving her my best breathing technique. "Close your eyes," I instruct. She obeys, her eyelids fluttering like trapped moths. "In for five seconds, hold for five seconds, out for ten seconds, all the while you imagine the stress is little butterflies fluttering out of your lungs and up and away."

As we walk through the visualization, I watch her shoulders relax. When her eyelashes finally waver open, the glossy sheen in her eyes is gone. She doesn't offer a smile, but she lets out a pretty solid sigh. "Thanks." Her voice drops from a frantic squeak into something more controlled, and she proceeds to gather her bag.

"It's my pleasure." Despite my diligence to avoid looking at the clock in front of students, my gaze slides to my wall clock. We're minutes away from the final bell. I can't help but let out a sigh too. She gives a singular nod before slipping out the door, and I wave at her until she's around the corner. I stay exactly where I am, the professional mask slipping enough to feel the ache in my own jaw from clenching it.

Replying to my own advice in my head, I try to visualize butterflies carrying my stress out of my lungs, but the air in my chest is wet cement. Everything I tell myself to picture just feels like I'm kicking more rocks into the pile. It doesn't work for me the way it worked for her, and I'm fed up. I lean back in my chair, rubbing at the tension in my neck as the last bell finally rings. One thing is becoming clearer than ever. After the "time off" I took this summer, I'm still not feeling better.

If anything, I'm feeling worse.

I'm the woman with all the answers for everyone else and not a clue how to fix my life. I tell kids every day they need to communicate, to take responsibility for their choices, to fight for what matters.

And yet—*me*?

I ran away.

And like I predicted: running away didn't solve anything, because all my problems stayed right where they were, completely unsolved and waiting for me.

My phone buzzes with a reminder, which causes me to leak a dark chuckle. "Homecoming Committee meeting, 3:30 p .m." Of course. Because nothing says *putting myself first* like spending the weekend chaperoning the school dance for kids who aren't even my kids. I shake my head, grab my planner, and whisper to myself, "Do as I say, not as I do." However, that needs to change...

Twelve

BLAKE

My phone rests in the perfect center of the desk like a live wire, evidence of the three-month standoff. All summer I'd imagined the speech she'd give. Surely, she'd come back with an apology for overreacting. But the house stayed quiet, and my armor of pride eventually just became a cage. Now, the weight in my chest has shifted from a dull ache to a sharp, constant throb. I can't take it anymore. If I don't get some relief, I'll have a medical emergency. My thumb hovers over her name, trembling enough to be pathetic. For ten agonizing minutes, I stare at the "Call" button like it's the only shred of hope I have left. I swallow the last of my ego. It's a bitter pill when I press my thumb on her name.

Pitiful.

I own a gym, run a media company, and bench-press more than most of my guys can squat, but dialing my own wife's number has me sweating like a rookie before his first game. I'm also appropriately wearing black workout gear today, as if I'm ready to attend my own funeral. Maybe it's too soon to reach out? The worst thing that can happen is she takes out a restraining order, but I'm so over this separation, I'm ready to risk it all. "Lacey?" My voice comes out squeaky, but I'm proud I manage to say anything.

The pause is long enough for me to picture her debating whether or not to hang up. My gut knots as I wait. "Hi, Blake." She's polite with the same tone she uses when she talks to students.

Craving a fidget, I rub a hand over my unshaven jaw. "How was your first week back at school?"

"Busy," she maintains her even voice. "Enrollment is up, as usual. It seems like the district's only solution is to keep packing students into classrooms. It's getting harder for kids to get the schedules they want, which leads to drama I get sucked in to, but I guess that's good job security for me. The good news is everyone survived.

"You always were good at your job." The words slip out before I can stop them. She doesn't reply, and I scream at myself for saying something that sounds like a compliment. They feel off-limits now. Like they offend her. Clearing my throat, I push through the butterflies ripping in my gut. "Listen, it's been a while. I'm sorry if you were waiting for me to call you, but you said you needed space. I was doing my best to respect that, but I'm wondering if we could meet up to talk about things. I could take you to dinner or coffee, or whatever works for you?"

"Blake." Her voice softens, but it's not the softness I want. "I don't know if that's a good idea."

I grip the phone tighter. "I understand needing a break, but we can't go on like this forever. We can't pretend this is normal."

I hear the hitch in her breath before she admits, "I don't know what I'd say." She sighs, loud and long. "I feel like every time I've tried to communicate with you, we end up right back in the same fight. I'm seriously out of answers about what to do next. Fighting has never helped us."

"Then let's not fight," I say quickly. "Let's just talk, or you can talk, and I will agree not to say anything back. I can smile at you. Unless smiling is illegal. I can stare at the corner."

Silence penetrates through the phone; louder than if she were screaming at me. I shift my weight from foot to foot. "I'll think about it."

My gaze lowers to the floor as a solid mass swells in my throat. I so badly want my wife back in my life. I desperately want to fix it. I wasn't prepared for this fight to last this long. I'm not a quitter when it comes to fighting for what I want, but this is so different. I don't know how to move forward if she doesn't agree to talk to me. "Okay, think about it all you need. May I text you tomorrow to see how you feel?"

"Fine, Blake, if you're going to insist, let's have dinner tomorrow. It probably is time for us to talk about some things, but that's all we're doing. Just talking. Don't expect me to come home," she rushes out. Before I can say anything, the line goes dead. Shaking my head, I stare at the wall as my head spins. My thoughts circle back to the trap it's been stuck in for months. I don't know if I'm winning her back or just learning how far gone she already is.

But I'm not giving up.

Thirteen

Lacey

It's two adults, who share children, meeting to figure out the logistics of life. I breathe out an easy breath as I hype myself up. Paisley mentioned the other day her assignment with Granite Ice is almost over. She hasn't been able to cover her bills on her own, and it's been nice for her having Blake help with that while she's working for him. Not to mention Peyton never returned to college. He's still living in the apartment with Paul and Preston, who are both still playing college hockey. I'm sure Blake's funding Peyton's share still. I'm sure we need to start talking about who is helping which child and how much.

It's been a long time since Blake and I sat down together to intentionally talk. If I had to look back, I'd say the lack of meaningful conversation is the one thing that started my spiral. Blake was always content to come home, take his smelly gym shirt off, plop down on the couch, and zone out. Oh, but not before he made it to the fridge to retrieve the healthy dinner I home cooked for him and saved. He wouldn't even mutter a thank you. It was like he thought we had some magic dinner fairy who stocked the fridge and also made the dishes disappear out of the sink.

Before I knew it was happening, years of begging for connection turned into me constructing walls to protect my heart from constant disappointment. I'm not ready to tear down those walls just because Blake asked me to have one dinner. Nope. He needs to try harder than that. Still, I change my blouse twice, and the confusion over my wardrobe has me reminiscing about the first time Blake and I hung out all those years ago at my prom. I chose blue that day because it was the safe choice. Today, I also settle on a soft blue. It's always a safe choice.

Blake let me pick the restaurant, and I deliberately avoided any of our favorite places that would spark memories and any place that feels like a date spot. I want bright lighting and people bustling everywhere. A place where you get in and out quickly, but I also don't want him to think I'm low effort. I'm done with the fast meals we don't enjoy together. With that in mind, I carefully selected an Irish pub on the corner of Main Street. It's well known for its excellent cuisine and friendly atmosphere.

Arriving right on time, I see myself inside and stand in the foyer, looking around at the wood décor. The place feels a bit like a maze with its low ceilings and dark mahogany. It's funny how when I walk into the room, I can feel Blake before I spot him. Even from across the pub, we are so in tune to each other's presence, my eyes instantly land on his. He jumps to his feet with a boyish grin planting on his face as he calls my name. It seems cute, but I have to believe it's a ploy to keep me from turning around and leaving.

I steel my shoulders back and take my time strolling over while unguarded heat floods my cheeks from the smile he's giving me. It feels a little too late. On the plus side, at least he knows I'm here. In the past, he would have his face plastered to the TV and whatever sports game was playing. Not this time. And I don't know if I'm upset or happy about it.

"Lacey," he says in a lower tone, as I reach the high-top table. He wobbles on his feet like he doesn't know if he should hug me or just nod. Keeping my gaze low, I straddle my stool before he tries to touch me. "Thanks for coming," he says as he sits back down and scoots his stool closer.

I shrug. "Well, with four kids, we are going to need to talk to each other."

My hands stay neatly folded in my lap, as if I'm sitting through a quarterly performance review with my boss instead of dinner with a man who I once thought I'd spend forever with. Avoiding his direct eye contact, I glance over at the bar, where a young couple leans toward each other as if the rest of the room has faded away. The woman wears a deep red dress that hugs her curves. Her hair falls in loose waves, catching the warm light like copper. She's the perfect picture of youth and beauty. When she lifts a fork, she offers a bite of her wedge of chocolate cake to the man. He leans forward, and she proceeds to feed him. The fork isn't even out of his mouth before he laughs until his eyes crinkle. The sound of young love lands in my chest with a gentle ache that reminds me of when Blake used to sit too close at tables. Being a professional athlete, he never splurged on dessert, but he was guilty of sharing my fries. On those dates, we'd share more than food, as it seemed like we could trade our deepest secrets just by locking eyes. My gut twists with all the memories that beg to be recalled, but I smash them down.

The silence stretches long enough to scrape against my nerves before Blake clears his throat. "So, I can't remember the last time it rained this much in September."

My lips twitch as if they've forgotten how to smile at Blake. It's been so long since we've tried to do this conversation stuff.

It's wild that it took me to move out for an entire summer to finally get him to try. "At least it's not snow, right?"

His gaze flicks briefly toward the window next to us before landing back on me. "You always said you loved the smell after it rains."

Shocking that he remembers.

That one doesn't feel fair though. I talked about it for twenty-five years. He smiles fondly at me like it doesn't kill his soul to remember the small things. "Yes." I'm careful to avoid eye contact. He doesn't need to see how truly hard this is for him to show up now, after all the years of begging.

The waiter appears, wearing jeans and a casual red polo shirt. He lays laminated menus on the table, with a tablet in his other hand, ready to punch in our orders. Before I can open my menu, Blake starts ordering. "She'll have the salmon," he says, not even glancing at me. "And I'll take the ribeye with baked potato. Medium."

My fingers graze at the edge of my menu as I study him, wondering what in the world is going on? Blake used to order for me when we were dating. Back then it felt thoughtful. It was in the days before menus were online, and he'd call the restaurants ahead of our date and ask what the specials were. He'd make reservations at the place with my favorite food and always insisted I get the best. I felt so seen back then. It was also comfortable, like he was taking a chore off my back. He'd always order the most expensive thing that he knew I'd enjoy.

As time went on, he stopped doing that. He'd stare at his phone while I studied the menu, doing mental math in my head to make sure our bill wasn't going to be too high. It's crazy how losing that gesture added to the feelings of being invisible. Until the day came where we stopped going out to eat because I didn't care to stare at him staring at his phone.

Why would he remember to do it now?

My brain floods with emotions. Confusion, anger, and maybe even a tad bit of happiness, like there's a shred of hope for us if he can remember these things after all these years. My mouth goes dry from being overwhelmed.

And the truth is, he got my order perfect.

Maybe it should feel controlling, but a flutter that has no business being here rises in my gut. I hate how my body responds to him, even when I'm begging it not to. I press my knees tighter together under the table and reply, "That's fine."

But it isn't fine.

Not even close to fine.

I don't think I'll ever understand how a man who can look at any menu and know exactly what I would love could grow so distant. We became strangers who slept in the same bed. The waiter takes our menus back and walks away. Blake looks over the table at me, a little sheepishly. "You look pretty."

Heat creeps up my neck, despite the fact his compliment feels ten years overdue. I reach for my water glass and take slow sips as I search for something safe to talk about. "So, have you heard from Paisley?" I stay with something safe.. "I know you sent her on assignment for the magazine, but I know it's coming to an end."

"It's not over yet." A smile tugs at his mouth. "I'll admit when she decided not to go to college, it upset me, but now that I have her interning, I want to give her as much experience as I can. It can only help her in the long run."

"Right." I chew my bottom lip for a beat. "Just as long as you don't wear her out."

The waiter returns faster than I'd expected, and he sets down my salmon, and I gape at it. Somewhere in the last ten minutes, this fish has become some weird symbol of all the ways Blake and I lost connection.

"So," He exhales a deep breath as he cuts into his steak. "I assume you have a nice place to stay?"

"An Airbnb for now." I keep my tone clipped. "It's sure quiet."

"That's good." He shifts in his seat with his fork and his knife in his hands, but he hasn't taken a bite yet. His gaze holds on me, which again feels like an insult. For so many years, I pleaded for him to put his stupid phone down and have a normal dinner conversation, but he couldn't. Even though he's looking at me now, I can't focus. All I see is the flashback of him watching hockey while I blink tears back. "You always said you wanted quiet," he says.

I finally glance up, narrowing my eyes. "Right, usually the TV was blaring so loudly with a game, I couldn't hear myself think."

A corner of his mouth lifts. "I mean, you did marry a hockey player."

I pretend to need to focus on my fork, stabbing my fish without even cutting it. "This isn't—"

"I know." His voice is softer now. "We don't need to bicker, but I don't think we should act like strangers either."

That lands too close to my heart, twisting it into a knot. We've been strangers for years. He's just finally noticing it. I'm so over trying to reverse it; I change the subject. "How is the gym?"

He leans back, the proud-owner smirk flashing across his face. "It's always going well. Peyton's working, and bringing in younger members. If it keeps growing at this rate, I'll be looking to add an expansion for more group fitness classrooms or maybe look at another location."

"That's good," I say it, and I mean it. For all his flaws, I've always admired his drive. But part of me aches too, because this is the version of Blake I fell for: passionate, ambitious, alive. I miss when I felt included in all of that. I look down, tracing the rim of my plate with my finger. It's crazy how I have no appetite for the food in front of me. I was starving all day. Now that I'm here, I can barely look at it. A wave of nausea rolls up my stomach. Before I know it, I gag. I push my stool back quickly, clutching my napkin like a shield. "Excuse me," I whisper. "I'm feeling ill."

Swiftly, he slides from his stool and stands. "Can I walk you to the bathroom?"

"No, I think I need to leave. I'm sorry, but this isn't going to work." My hands shake as I grab my purse and sling it over my shoulder, already striding toward the door as tears well in my eyes. No matter how hard I pretend otherwise, I'm not as detached as I want to be.

Not even close.

Until I heal, these types of "get-togethers" aren't going to happen again.

Fourteen

BLAKE

Hours after our dinner, I'm wired and lying wide awake in bed. Every word of Lacey's plays on a loop in my head. It was a short dinner, and she left early, even before she finished her meal. Some guys might focus on that as a bad thing. I don't see it that way at all. The fact she showed up, looking so pretty, feels like proof she hasn't shut me out completely.

I roll onto my side and shut my eyes. When I still can't sleep, I sit up, muttering, "Screw this. I might as well be productive and call the only other insomniac I know." I grapple for my phone on my nightstand and hit "Call." I stand up and pace to my office, waiting. Paisley answers on the fourth ring.

"Hey, Dad."

"Hey, honey, how's it going in Mapleton?"

"Good," she says a little too carefully that it leans more on the sus side. "Actually, really good." Her tone is soaked in something that makes my stomach drop. I know that sound. I've heard it before. Shoot, I chased it with her mother for years.

"Good *how*?" My voice comes out sharper than I mean. To cool my already rising temper, I allow my thumb to rhythmically trace the edge of my phone case. It's not a nervous habit or anything, but more of something to stop me from ruining this conversation before I find out all I need to know. I trace the edge over and over as I wait for her to reply. I can almost picture her chewing her lower lip. When my impatience finally bubbles over, I breathe out, "Are you still there?"

"I'm here," she delays again before adding, "I just...I don't know if I have the right words for this yet."

Hiking a brow out of curiosity, I downplay how nervous her hesitation is making me. We've never been as close as the boys, but she's never acted scared to talk to me before. "Paisley, if you're in trouble, don't be afraid to tell me. I'm only here to—"

"I've been spending a lot of time with one of the players. We went skiing—"

The words slam into me right as I get to my office, and I freeze in the doorway. My chest tightens. "You're *dating* one of Bill's players?"

"Dad, that's not what I said. Spending time is not the same as dating—"

"No. Absolutely not. That's a conflict of interest. You're supposed to be covering them, not—"

"I'm living my own life!" Her voice suddenly becomes fierce. "And he's not who you think he is."

"Don't tell me I don't know his type," I bite out. "They're all the same! Arrogant, selfish, on and off the ice. I've seen it a thousand times."

"This isn't about you!" she fires back. "This is about me. For once, can you stop trying to control everything about everyone else, and look at your own life!"

My fingers clench around the phone so hard, it starts to shake. I fight to hold back all the words I want to say, because I know if I speak now, I'll be full-blown yelling.

She sighs, softer now but it does nothing to ease the tension. "I have to go." The line goes dead, and I sit here, staring into the dark.

First my wife.

Now my daughter.

Bill's shadow forever stretches over my life.

Sure, I'm not perfect, but why is this happening again?

I should have known better than to send my daughter to Bill Baker. I thought she had a good head and could see through the lies. She's not like most girls. She's not one to get all swoony eyed over hockey players. She's not one to date much, at all. She's an intellectual, and she grew up with hockey, as all her brothers played. Not once in all those games did she ever show any interest in the game or a player. I honestly thought she was immune to it. Leave it to Bill to lure my precious daughter into his claws.

I'm still clenching my phone, but I don't want to risk accidentally on purpose chucking it at the wall, as I have a deep craving to throw something. I carefully walk forward and slide it on my desk and take a step back. My gaze pivots back to the Granite Ice logo target on my wall, and my eyes narrow until my vision blurs.

Bill is going to pay for this!

It's only fair.

Fifteen

LACEY

I bought another plant.

Okay, okay, I'm not proud of it.

I don't know what came over me. I couldn't help myself. I was in the grocery store, minding my own little business while I tried to find the best deal on coffee. Out of the corner of my eye, I noticed a lovely orchid with beautiful ivory blooms, and I walked right up to it like it needed a hug. Before I knew it, it was in my cart. I took it to my office as I hope seeing it every day will remind me to water it, but I can't help but think something deeper is going on.

Plus, now it's like staring at me.

I'm reviewing my notes for a college prep workshop, and my gaze keeps sliding back to the orchid like it's judging me for not taking it back to the house I own with my husband. Like plants even know about home ownership or spouses. It's this weird mind trap. I'm actually relieved when my phone lights up.

Well, relief that dies too quickly.

It's Blake.

I consider letting it ring out. After meeting up with him the other night, I've decided to keep my distance. Nothing went terribly wrong. I thought I'd made progress and would be able to see him without it tearing open my wounds, but the opposite happened. When he so easily ordered my food like he knew it was something I appreciated but yet for so long he forgot to care about me, it felt like he'd purposely chose to ignore me. He knew how to show up for me, but he clearly just didn't want to. Now, I'm back to overanalyzing things, and my head throbs. Maybe healing for me doesn't mean I'll ever make it back home. Maybe it means I put myself first while staying far, far away from him, while I engage in my new plant hoarding hobby.

The phone rings and rings. It should go to voicemail any second. I hold my breath waiting for it to stop, but the mother part of me, who worries it might be something about one of the kids, makes me grapple for the phone at the very last second and swipe to answer. "Hey," I say cautiously.

"Lacey." His voice is raw. "I just got off the phone with Paisley."

Immediately, my stomach tightens. "What happened?"

"She's seeing one of Bill Baker's players." The word *players* comes out like venom.

I close my eyes, pressing my hand against my forehead. Oh, wow, that's interesting. Paisley's never had a boyfriend, and Blake tends to exaggerate. It might not be that bad. "Well, it's probably not serious, but maybe she's happy?"

"You think?" His frustration crackles through the line. "I don't want her to get hurt. You know what those guys are like."

"I know," I whisper, not adding another word. I know all about it. I've lived it. But again, Paisley is smart. She's not one to rush into things. "Seeing" doesn't imply an exclusive commitment. It could mean so many things. Blake is likely overreacting.

"I told her it was a mistake," he says, his voice breaking a little. "But she won't hear it from me."

"You know she's her own person." I lean back in my chair and settle in, as this conversation is already lasting longer than I'd like. "Wonder where she gets that from."

The smallest chuckle bleeds over the phone before his tone shifts into something unguarded, and he rushes out, "Lacey, I hate doing this alone. I miss you."

My breath catches.

"I miss us," he continues, the words tumbling out now like he can't hold them in. "The way it used to be before everything got so complicated. I miss waking up with you next to me, your advice even when I didn't want to hear it. I just—" His voice hitches. "I love you. And I wish we could just do life together again."

Hot tears well in the back of my eyes, blurring my vision. I don't exactly fight them because I'm alone in my office. Honestly, it feels good to have a release of pressure, but I swipe at them uselessly. "Blake," I say his name to fill in the silence, but I stop speaking because my heart is twisting. I want to tell him I feel the same, because that's what I begged for from him for years—to do this life together.

But the walls I built are solid.

Frankly, I don't believe if I come back right now, he'll be fully changed. Sure, he'll make an effort for a few days. Everything will eventually return to the way it was. I'm not playing games. I don't wish him any heartbreak. I truly need to move on from the constant heartache and disappointment, because it's crushing me. I know the statistics. I'm a counselor. Women who live in these kinds of marriages eventually get sick, and they get all the immune disorders. I'm not saying

I'm dying, but with almost daily headaches, I need to do what I can to preserve my own sanity so I can be present in my kids' lives.

And it's time I be present in my own life too. I'm not sure living with Blake allows me to do that. I was a ghost of a person when I lived in that house. "I don't know if we can go back," I whisper.

"I'm not asking to go back to the way it was," he says fiercely. "I'm asking for a chance to move forward."

Raising my gaze to the heavens, I pray silently, *God help me, I want to believe him, but I don't.* "I need to go, Blake. I'm still at the office." I barely get the words out, and my voice cracks with tears. I quickly end the call. Blake's words linger, echoing in my chest like bells. *I love you. I wish we could just do life together.*

I sit frozen as my vision continues to blur with tears I can't stop. Giving up on swiping them away, as they only fall harder, I drop my head into my hands and pray through my sobs.

God, why is he trying to change now? Why after all the years of begging, finally giving up, and deciding I need to heal, is he finally acting like he hears me? I walked away for a reason. I need to move forward. I can't go back.

And yet...

He sounds exactly like the person I knew he could be if he wanted to.

I curl my legs up under me on the chair, hugging them close like I'm trying to comfort myself. *Maybe he's changed?*

One thing terrifies me more than I ever thought; my heart never stopped loving him. I don't think I'll ever fully erase the love I have for him. The problem is that loving him has only hurt me.

And I'm tired of that.

That's what I cling to as I swipe at my tears again, clearing my face.

I've made a decision.

I need to stick with it.

I'll adjust. I just need some time.

Sixteen

BLAKE

By the time I hang up the phone, my lower jaw trembles.

Lacey cried. She fought hard to conceal it, but I heard it. She clearly misses me, even if she can't say it yet.

She still loves me.

I know it.

And I'm done sitting around waiting for someone else to write the ending to *our story*. Maybe I put off my marriage too much.

Okay, not maybe. Absolutely guilty.

That has to stop now before I lose the shot forever. Adrenaline races through my veins as my brain fires. Between my daughter falling for one of Bill's players and the hope of Lacey still loving me, I can't sit around. I pace the length of my office, plotting something to win back my wife and to get Paisley away from Bill's team.

And to win against Bill Baker.

He's had his slimy fingerprints all over my life for far too long.

Not anymore.

But what can I do?

My gaze lands on the framed photo I keep in the corner of my desk. It's my gym's opening day and my lips tip up into a slight smirk, as they always do when I recall the feeling of owning something I built with my bare hands after years of dreaming and planning. I got to stand proud in front of a crowd, knowing I'd made it happen. That day, everyone was proud of me.

That day, I won.

But now Bill had to go and ruin everything by one-upping me when he created a whole AHL team, making him on top, but that doesn't mean he has to stay there. I could totally get my own team. An even better team...

My gaze drops to the floor as an idea slowly rolls in.

That's it.

That's the answer!

I won't just cover sports. I'll *own* sports. Bill isn't the only guy who can start an AHL team. I'll build something bigger than his arena, better than his team, and more amazing than anything he's touched. I'll start my own AHL team right here on Long Island, and I'll use my magazine to catapult them to stardom. Bill won't know what hit his little team. And what if…I can steal some of his guys?

The ideas surge through me, wild and electric.

Wait!

Not just some of them. What if I can steal the guy Paisley is dating? Then there won't be a giant wedge between us that I know will be there if she gets serious with this guy.

I'm an absolute genius!

Call me Einstein.

Better yet, Anton-stein, with my own theory.

Is it risky? Yes.

Expensive? So much so it makes me sweat.

Borderline insane? Yeah, but it's the kind of insane I thrive on.

The kind of insane only a desperate man would do.

If Einstein rewrote time, Anton-stein rewrites the rules, and the first one, that my wife falls in love with me again, even if it makes me look like the most desperate man on the planet.

Am I desperate?

Yes, that's my new middle name, and I'm proud of it.

Blake Desperate Anton-stein.

I can already see it: my name on the jerseys, Paisley working alongside me instead of against me with Bill, and my beautiful and amazing wife in the stands, cheering us on.

The path ahead doesn't feel like a battle I'm losing.

It feels like a game I can win.

Bill's been lucky so far, but he's about to find out, he can't have all the luck.

Not when he's up against me.

I'll win them both back—my daughter and my wife—even if it kills me.

Pushing the pads of my fingers together, I flex my hands as I think. A mischievous grin splits my face. Why didn't I think of this sooner?

Seventeen

Lacey

It's a Wednesday night, and I've stayed late to work, partly because it's easier to concentrate after the last echoes of students fade. Also, partly because I've learned I don't care for hanging out in an empty house, and maybe also partly because *I bought another plant!*

It was a mistake. I knew it from the moment I walked into the greenhouse, but I was looking for some fertilizer for my orchid. I'm not going to do this plant mama thing in vain. I purposely went over my lunch break, so I'd be pressed for time. With a laser focus, I even kept on my sunglasses, but once I passed through the front door, that earthy aroma hit me right away. I was sucked in. One blink of an eye, and my gaze dropped to the cutest little pot of succulents. They really can't be much trouble at all as there are four different ones all in the same pot. My mama heart melted as it reminded me of my four kids. How each one is so different, but when you put them all in the same container, it's the best combination.

Anyway, he's on my desk now, sitting next to his brother, the orchid.

And is it bad I feel like I have to hang out later so he doesn't feel like I'm ditching him on the first night in his new home? Something is clearly wrong with me, but it's not like I don't have a mountain of work to do while I'm here.

So, I'm typing up college recommendations for a couple of my favorite seniors. It's easier to focus on other people's futures than my own. Yes, I know that sounds like a bit of a bigger issue that might be connected to my co-dependent plant issue, but at least for right now, I prefer to be *leafed* alone with my bad decisions. My phone buzzes, and a smile grows on my lips when I see it's my sister. "Hey," I say cheerfully.

"Have you heard what people are saying about you?"

"Ah," I deadpan as my mind goes blank. That's never a good start. My gaze slams to my plant siblings. Is my issue really that obvious? And she's all the way in Mapleton so how would she know? With a still expression, I take the bait, "What is it?"

"Your husband—I mean, ex, or separated, whatever, Blake. He's starting a hockey team. The online gossip is crazy. He's already got investors, city council talks scheduled, an arena proposal. He's clearly lost his mind, but I guess it's happening."

Tilting my head to the side, I stare at the peeling paint on the wall in front of me.

She's got the wrong Blake.

Blake wouldn't start a hockey team.

That's not just big.

That's massive.

That's insane.

"Are you sure you got the right dude?" I half laugh. "Blake has a gym and a sports magazine. I don't think he'd have time for a hockey team." I throw out my hand in a questioning gesture as I ask the next question more to myself, "And why would he even want to do that?"

"Yeah, I know who your husband—ex, person, dude is," she goes on. "It's him, and yeah, he has a hockey team."

"There's no way," I mutter as I go to my keyboard and type his name into my Google bar. I hit search, expecting to see all the typical headlines about his gym or even old hockey stats, but the first thing that pops up is a headline of him at some press conference. There's a fresh photo, and his eyes blaze with that familiar fire, the one that used to scare me as much as it thrilled me.

And just like that, I'm seventeen again, watching him storm into the rink with that same defiant grin, like the world was his for the taking. Only this time, the stakes are higher.

This isn't just a boy chasing a dream.

It's my husband risking *everything*.

Like everything.

Is he trying to go bankrupt?

Is that his plan so there's nothing for me? Is this to get revenge on me?

We are separated but nothing has been legal yet, as I've been trying to avoid taking it that far. All our finances are still completely connected. His money is my money.

My stomach knots.

I've always loved his drive, but I've never wanted to scream more than I do now. This reckless dreaming and unrelenting hours of work is exactly what tore us apart. I jerk my gaze away from the screen and return it back to the peeling wall paint. I breathe and try to center myself. "Yes, that's him," I say in a low voice as Lori has stayed mute, seemingly waiting for my reaction. "If I had to guess, this is his swan song. He's either going to win it all or lose everything trying."

I suppose I should find the team an odd project for him, but I don't. Blake has always been extreme. He believed in living the kind of life that was big. He has a successful gym, but that's only after years of working and neglecting his family. He has a successful magazine now. Again, because he sacrificed every human relationship he had to get it. The question isn't whether the third time is the charm. He's so stubborn, it will be a success. The question is, will he run our family out of money?

Lori cuts into my thoughts, "Well, I'm on my way out for the night. I hope that wasn't bad news for you."

"No, not bad. Just maybe suffocating." I throw my hand up as if I'm giving up. "But thanks for the FYI."

"Night." We hang up, and I'm left alone staring at my phone. I had told myself not to call him. He'll only get the wrong idea, but if I know Blake he doesn't ease into anything. He obsesses at an all-consuming level, sometimes pouring all our money into a new project, where I would have no money for groceries. Maybe that was okay when we were younger, but I want to retire someday. I can't risk losing everything now. There's a niggling in the back of my head that says I need to know what he's up to. Before I lose my nerve, I grab my phone and text:

> Hey, I hope it's not a bother, but I'm stopping at the house on the way home from work to grab a few more of my things.

Holding my phone out in front of me, I wait for it to light up with a return text. If I really wanted some things from the house, I'd sneak in when I knew he was at the gym. I sure wouldn't give him a heads-up. This is me reaching out without saying I'm reaching out. A moment later, I get my text.

Sure, I'm actually on my way home too. I'll see you there.

He never had that sense of urgency to see me before. Half the time he wouldn't reply to my texts for hours. Resisting the urge to roll my eyes, I push back my chair, gather my things for the night, wave goodbye to my plant siblings—because that's what good plant mamas do—and I lock my office behind me. As much as I told myself I don't want to see him again so soon, the house feels like a neutral zone where it's safe enough to talk. It's still my house too. I'm not exactly agreeing to meet him as I am grabbing a spare toothbrush.

I'm calm on the drive over, and I enter through the front door with my key, where Blake's waiting in the foyer for me. I'm taken back by the way his eyes are lit, burning with that same energy I saw in the news article. He's always had a spark for life. Lately, I've only ever seen that spark about his gym and his magazine. It certainly was never aimed at me until we met recently at the pub, which frankly scared me too much to think about.

"I'm starting a hockey team," he blurts out as soon as I'm over the threshold. I pinch back a smirk, as he fell right into my trap to get all the details. I didn't even have to fish for anything.

I blink at him, slowing my reaction to pretend I'm hearing about it for the first time. "A hockey team?"

"An AHL team." His mouth curves into that cocky grin that undid me in high school. "I've already got investors, and we've signed a contract on a warehouse off the interstate. We're converting it to an arena. It's happening, Lacey. We're going to have a team."

My heart lurches as he spills his dreams so openly to me, like he's already forgotten *we* aren't supposed to be doing things together anymore. Sure, I want the details, but I thought he'd be a little coy about it. He's literally standing in front of me with the proudest smile on his face, saying the word *"we're"* and including me in this. "Blake, *we're*—" I stop myself before saying the word *not*. I know Blake too well. To him, that word would only mean *challenge accepted*.

"We're," he echoes where I left off. His eyes fixed on me like I'm the only thing in the world that matters. My face burns because it's the way I yearned to be looked at for years. "I know what you're thinking," he goes on. "I'm insane, and

I can't get enough hockey, but this isn't about hockey. It's about our family."

"Blake." My throat tightens as the air is too heavy to swallow. This man only thinks in one color: hockey. Our family doesn't need a hockey team. Our family is fine. It's our marriage that died. If I know anything with one-hundred-percent certainty, it's our marriage is not in need of a hockey team. Maybe some flowers every few months or a dinner for two, but no, it will never require a hockey team. If anything, less hockey is what our marriage needs.

His eyes widen, sparkling in a vulnerable way I almost don't recognize. "Lacey, one thing about me is, I won't ever lie down and accept losing. I'm not losing our daughter to one of Bill's players. I have a plan to get her back here, but really, it's not even about that. All I want is my wife back. When I bring Paisley back, I'll prove to you finally how much this family has always been my number one priority. Sure, maybe it wasn't always clear, but I promise you, everything I've done, I've done with you guys in mind. I'm not losing you. I won't do it. I will die before I accept losing you."

The words pierce through every wall I've built these past years. My pulse hammers, traitorous tears stinging the backs of my eyes. I flash my gaze to the heavens and pray a silent prayer, *God help me, I believe he's serious about this because he's that crazy. I don't think I can handle this stress. I seriously just want a nice, quiet life. A hockey team? Ah, the drama that will bring*. This isn't putting another wedge between us. It's an arena with an entire team of men. I won't stand for it. I can't.

It's certainly not going to fix our marriage. I remember all the nights alone while he chased the last big thing. This isn't any different than the gym or the magazine. He says he loves me, but this isn't how you go about loving someone, or at least not me. It's not my love language. My hands twist together as I struggle with the words to tell him he's insane. I also don't want him to use it as fuel to try even harder. It's a delicate balance with him. "Blake, I understand what you think you're doing, but I don't need a hockey team. That's not my passion. I only participated because I loved you. I honestly don't know if love is enough this time. Frankly, I'm tired."

His jaw tightens, but his eyes—those stubborn, relentless eyes—don't waver. "Then I'll prove it is."

Looking away, I stare through the window and heave a heavy sigh. It's no use attempting to talk him into doing anything else. He will get this hockey team. Even though I don't understand how he thinks it will bring us back together. I also know he doesn't care that I don't understand. He does things his way. That's the real issue he will never understand.

We should do things *our* way.

Lowering my gaze to the floor, I side-step around him as I head upstairs to pretend to grab a few things. I can't talk to him anymore about this. As much as he says he's making progress, he doesn't understand at all. I highly doubt he ever will.

He's clueless.

Eighteen

Blake

It's hours before sunrise, and I'm back in the gym after staying late last night. I can't be at the house with Lacey not there. Besides, I get the best workouts before I unlock the door for everyone else to come in. It's just me and Peyton, who's been working the mornings with me. At first it enraged me that he left school. I paid so much money for him to study, and he quit right before he got his degree, but he's been showing up every day to help pay his rent.

Honestly, it's been nice having him here. He also comes early before his shift to work out, trying to stay in hockey shape as he looks for a job. We grind out all our stress on the bench. Today, the bar trembles above my face, and my arms shake with the last rep, but I love it. Peyton places a hand on the bar to steady it for me, his face serious with concentration. "C'mon, Dad. One more."

I grit my teeth, drive it upward, and the weight slams back onto the rack with a clang. Peyton smirks with the same cocky grin that used to stare back at me when I was his age. It doesn't feel like it was that long ago when I was twenty-two. Time sure flies. I had the whole world at hand, and a bright future ahead of me. Now I can't breathe normally. Shaking my head, I push out the negative thoughts, as I know that's the reason my muscles are so tight today. "Thanks for the spot."

The front door wafts open, sparking my attention. It's way too early for my regulars to come in, so I twist my head. Paisley's stalking toward me. Her dark hair is pulled back in a messy bun, and she's wearing a loose sweatshirt over leggings. I don't miss her sharp eyes that are lasered in on me.

Of course, I'm happy to see she's left Mapleton. But something tells me *everything* is off. She doesn't ever work out at my gym. She's here for another reason. My stomach drops. "Squirt." I frown when nothing about her expression says she's happy to see me. "I told you to let me know when you got on the road." I curl my fingers back around the bar and push up.

"I knew I wouldn't be able to sleep, so I ended up driving home last night." She crosses her arms over her chest and juts out her foot in another gesture that tells me she's not happy.

"That's good," I speak on my exhale and then pause before I lower the bar. "Glad you made it home safe."

Peyton counts out my reps, and I wait for Paisley to express what's on her mind, but she's quiet. Eventually she steps to the side and finds a treadmill to walk on, which is so odd.

Maybe she's not upset?

I steal a glance over my shoulder, and she's watching the TV, looking content. I finish my workout in silence, as neither Peyton nor I have ever been much for talking. After a few minutes, I see Paisley scurry to the locker room and then speedwalk back across the gym with her gaze focused on the exit like she's avoiding me. "Hey, Paisley," I call out as I sit up. She glances over her shoulder, and I tack on, "Where are you headed?"

"Ah, I have things to do." She drops her gaze to the floor and says, "And I want to quit the magazine."

Peyton, who remains by my side, blurts out, "Is this about Noah?"

"Maybe." Paisley's gaze focuses above us. "What do you think?"

I shake my head and dab at my temples with a towel. "I think…" I pause because it's a struggle to not yell how much I hate Bill Baker for stealing my only daughter. Instead of screaming, I twist the towel lengthwise and wrap it around my neck, slowly raising my gaze to hers as I'm terrified to see what she's really thinking. My heart plummets when I see a gleam in her eyes. With eyes that twin with Lacey's, I've seen that exact same gleam every time Lacey told me she loved me. She was fearless and didn't care who she upset by loving me, which made me love her even more. Together we were unstoppable. Ice runs through my veins. I never expected my daughter to repeat my wife's pattern. Swallowing, I force my voice not to crack. "I think that boy's trouble, but I can see by the spark in your eye you're going to love him anyway."

"Maybe you're right." Her eyes flash, just like her mother's when she's had enough. She offers a weak shoulder shrug before adding, "But I think I need to find out for myself."

The words slice clean through me. My jaw locks, and she spins on her heel and leaves.

Peyton shifts uncomfortably, looking at me, waiting for my explosion. But I don't have one. I can't. Not now. "Dad?" he finally asks with a low voice.

I wipe my face with the edge of a towel, force a grin I don't feel, and clap my hands together. "Back to work. We've got a lot to do."

But inside, my chest aches. Paisley doesn't understand she's about to wreck her life.

And Bill's dark and ugly shadow looms over everything...

But not for long.

This isn't just about revenge anymore.

It's about taking back everything I've lost.

I swipe the rest of the sweat off my brow and hustle to my office to get ready for the next order of business on my to-do list. Raising money. I've tidied up the little conference room at the gym to welcome in my new best friend, Mr. Michaels, a local billionaire with so much money to waste, he could easily fund my whole team. He doesn't know we're best friends yet, but he will.

An hour later, he arrives just on time, and I shake his hand for the first time and usher him into my boardroom. My mission is to make him love me so much he opens his wallet. His tailored suit and straight expression tell me it's not going to be so easy.

He sits in the seat closest to the door, and I sit across from him. I've never been good with words as I'm an all-action guy, but I'm not letting my fears hold me back. I lean forward and keep my voice even. "Thank you for coming." I want him to know I'm serious and all business. Refusing to waste his time, I cut right to the chase, "I know what you're thinking. Why put your money in someone who's not in the game anymore?"

He shifts like he's ready to agree with that statement.

I slam my hand on the table. "Because no one wants this more than I do! Because I know what it's like to be counted out. I know how to build from nothing. Look at this gym." I gesture to the open door behind me that leads to the weight room. "Look at the business I built and the athletes I've trained. This isn't theory. This is decades worth of grit. And I'm telling you this team will be the next big thing." I slide a folder of all my research across the table. "Take a look at the numbers."

If he thinks I'm insane, he doesn't hint at it, and he opens the folder and studies the first few sheets for what seems like a long time. I don't dare interrupt him. After the longest beat of silence, a smoldering bead of sweat springs on my brow. I don't wipe because I don't want to draw attention to it. When he looks me straight in the eye, I lock in on his words. "So far, I like what I see," he says. "Let me talk to my team. I'll definitely be in touch."

That's it.

No hard questions.

No excuses.

The man clearly knows how to make decisive decisions and not mess around.

He stands, not waiting for me to walk him out of the room. I rise to my feet but then freeze, as I'm not sure if I should spew some numbers at him or try to get him to stick around with a little small talk. I'm not good at this part. I've always done business all by myself, but if I'm going to get the kind of team I need to get, I need more money. "Thank you. I'm hosting drinks tonight for anyone who may have questions. I'll text you the details," I manage to say as I stand by the door and watch him exit. As soon as he's out of sight, I let out a sigh of relief.

That was crazy.

I might have just made a multi-million-dollar deal, and it didn't even take fifteen minutes. This is really happening. I'm getting my team. Adrenaline surges through my extremities, and I want so badly to tell someone but being so early in the planning stages, I really need to keep things on the DL. Still, I pull my phone out of my pocket and look for any missed messages.

I know who I want to see on my phone, but she's not there. It's killing me. I so badly want to call her and tell her how my meeting went. I so badly miss the days when she was my person. My heart pounds in my chest. All I can think about is her. Everything I'm doing is *for* her. Always and forever will be hers. I open my text message and construct a text filled with everything I know to be true today and forever.

I love you. Always have, always will. No matter what.

I stare at the words for a second, thumb hovering. Then I hit "Send."

If I can win an investor who only knew me for fifteen minutes, I can win my wife of twenty-five years back too. It's simple math.

Nineteen

LACEY

If I don't mumble any words to properly introduce my new potted cactus to his two sibling plants, it will be like he doesn't exist. Tiptoeing, I cross my small office while tucking the brown paper bag in the crook of my arm, like I'm bootlegging moonshine into the school. I slide behind my desk, all the while I pinch back my dopamine-encrusted smile. Gingerly I remove the bright teal and coral striped ceramic pot from the paper bag and place it ever so quietly on the corner of my desk...stand back.

Yes!

Just as I predicted. He's the perfect shade of green to complement the other two. They really do resemble a family. Really, since he's a cactus, he basically needs no care. I hardly need to even water him. It's like a free space in Bingo. He's just there, brightening the room up with his cheery pot. If anything, it's healthy for me to have him, as he's cleaning my air. This has nothing to do with me avoiding anything, or...

"Mrs. Anton, I need to drop geometry," a male voice groans from my doorway.

Startling like I was in here doing something illegal, I straighten and my hands fly behind me. I glance up to see one of my sophomores, Braydon Wilson, peeking his head in my doorway. He shifts his weight from one foot to the other, like he's uncomfortable being near my office. With one eye on him and the other on my new plant—because I'm making sure he is comfortable where he is—I smile softly and gesture for him to sit in the armchair in front of my desk. "Hi, Braydon, tell me what's going on."

"It's just—" His words tumble out all at once. "I've never been good at math. I don't like it. My parents keep saying I should be able to handle it, but I don't understand any of it. No matter how long I study, I keep failing my assignments. And if I fail, my parents will freak. It's better if I quit now, so it doesn't go on my record. Can you just put me in Everyday Math Skills?" His voice trails off as his gaze drops to the floor.

I understand his feeling of failure, as once again, I check my plant siblings on my desk.

"Well, let's not give up yet. Maybe we can find something to help." I walk behind my desk and tap my mouse until my computer screen glows to life with a dozen open tabs cluttered across the top. It's just a normal day spent juggling other people's drama. "Let's see if there's a tutor available for you." I scroll through the screens until I land on a tutoring schedule. "What period is your study hall?"

"Second."

"Yeah." I place my finger on the screen, so he can see the open spot. "It looks like there's a few options for tutors available during second. Why don't I plug you in? You don't have to commit forever, but you can try it out and see how it goes. My guess is you just need a little more help, and there's nothing wrong with that."

"I mean, if you really think it's going to help." He watches me as I adjust his schedule.

"It's worth a shot, and you are all set, starting tomorrow. Instead of going to the library for study hall, report to the tutoring lab." I refresh my screen, and his new schedule populates in front of me, and on cue, he lets out a deep exhale.

"Thanks, I guess," he murmurs like he's still not convinced he can do any better, but I smile bigger at him.

"You'll get the hang of it. And, if you try this tutor out, and it's not a good fit for you, come back in. We'll try something else. There are all kinds of help available. We just need to find the right kind that works for you."

"Okay. Sounds good." He gets up and leaves, calling, "Thanks again," over his shoulder.

I lean back in my chair, staring at his schedule on my computer, feeling confused. It's funny how I can so easily tell these kids everything will work out, and they just need to keep trying, when I have a hard time believing my own advice.

My phone buzzes on the desk. I glance at it distractedly. What do you know, it's Blake.

> **I love you. Always have, always will. No matter what.**

The words punch the air from my lungs. "Seriously," I whisper as I pick up the phone and press the screen to my chest like it's a lifeline.

Because I want to believe him.

But believing him before nearly broke me. And I don't know if I can risk letting him close enough to do it again. It's so much easier to be a plant mama. My gaze slides to my growing desk garden, and I can't help but smirk. It's pretty drama free from where I'm sitting.

The bell rings, and instant chatter fills the hallway. I paste on a smile for the kids passing by my open door. I could easily get up and shut the door for some privacy, but when I accepted this position, I pledged to myself that my door would always be open for these students. They need to see that. For the most part, I've never broken that rule, except for when I've closed it to allow for a private conversation with a student.

Now as I stare out my door, it becomes a random metaphor for all that is unbalanced in my life. Sure, my door at work is always open, but I've long since slammed that door into my heart. Now that it's closed, I don't know how or if I even want to open it again. It's safer with it closed.

The second bell rings. Students clear out of the hall. Everything is quickly restored to quiet, which means I need to get back to work. My gaze floats back to my computer screen to check for my upcoming meeting, but I can't help but feel that text on my phone.

It's like it's speaking to me.

And I have a few minutes before my next student comes, so I grab my phone and type:

> **Blake, I love you too. I never stopped, and I don't think I ever will, but I can't do it anymore.**

I stare at the words, but to my surprise, I don't press "Send."

Instead, I delete the message letter by letter, until all that's left is a blank screen.

Why am I so stuck?

Blowing out a heavy breath, I set my phone down before I do anything crazy. I don't understand why I can't let myself love him again. I know the truth: I still love Blake. Yet something's still wrong inside me. I rub my temples where a familiar headache starts to throb. It's all the stress that comes from balancing work, years of raising kids, and now a separation.

I think of the advice I give every single day in this office. *Don't put yourself last. If something feels wrong, ask for help.* I've told that to a dozen kids this week alone. Maybe it's time I took my own words seriously? What if it is something more than just stress? I've been getting these migraines for months.

I pull up my calendar again on my computer, scrolling until I find a day that's not filled up. Then I pick up the phone and dial my doctor's office. Maybe the problem isn't just Blake? He's always been a faithful husband. I don't doubt he loves me. It shouldn't be so hard, and I shouldn't be stuck. Maybe the problem is me?

And I need to know the truth before I take this separation too far.

Or...I shoot a glance at my growing plant obsession—*collection* is the better word. Or the plant life slowly buries me alive in my office.

The following day, I take an hour of the over one thousand hours of sick leave I've banked from never taking a day off, and I do what I've been putting off for a while. It's not that I'm afraid of the doctor. I'm embarrassed I—a trained professional—have let my regular exams and appointments slide to the wayside for years under the pressure of raising a family and balancing a career. It's silly to be embarrassed. I know that, but I don't magically stop feeling that way because I tell myself to stop. Finally, after all of these years, I'm sitting on the edge of the exam table, and I let my feet dangle like I'm six instead of forty-something.

"Lacey Anton," Dr. Tang, my female family medical doctor, who I last saw many years ago, walks in. "It's great to see you. How are you?"

"Hi, Dr. Tang." My life feels so overwhelming that I can't stop my eyes from swelling round. She wants to know how I am? Where do I start? The headaches. The bone-deep exhaustion. I swallow hard, saying the only words I can find, "I don't really know how I am, to be honest. I know it sounds weird, but I don't feel like myself. I haven't for a long time."

Taking a seat on the rolling stool in front of the desk, she keeps her eyes locked on me. "Okay. That's a good start. Can you be more specific?"

"Well, I think the main thing is exhaustion. I'm at this point in my life where I have a very low tolerance for stress. I know what I should do to take care of myself, but I'm so tired all the time. I even took the entire summer off and stayed with my sister, thinking getting away would help, but it did nothing. My brain can't handle anything extra, which is why I'm way overdue to even come in for a checkup."

"Well, I'm glad you came to see me. Let me just check your labs quickly." Dr. Tang takes a minute to scroll through my chart on the computer, pauses, and gives me a pointed look. "It looks like it's been a long time since you've had blood work done. Anemia is always something to consider when dealing with exhaustion, but I don't care to speculate. I'd like to send you to the lab first. Once we get your blood, we can go from there. If anything, it will rule out a lot of easy things and hopefully point us in the right direction. Does that sound okay?"

"It sounds good." Something inside my chest loosens when she doesn't say it's all in my head. The fact she's taking me seriously gives me hope that maybe whatever is happening to me can be fixed.

She types a few notes into the computer and then stands. "Your lab orders are in. Head down now if you have time."

"Thank you." I force a tired smile.

"You are very welcome, and I will call you as soon as we have your results." She pauses to give me a smile, most likely the rehearsed one she gives all her patients, and then says, "Have a great day," and she exits the room.

I leave the office, feeling a tad hopeful. Not physically better, but lighter because I finally did what I would tell all my students to do. I asked for help.

That's a huge start.

Hopefully, it will lead me where I need to go to get better. My phone buzzes in my bag. A text from Blake, no doubt. Flashing my gaze to the heavens, I grumble under my breath, "He's relentless." Peeling back the zipper just enough to stick my hand inside, I reach in and silence my phone. With heavy feet and a worried heart, I'm off to the lab and then back to work.

"Sometimes," I say, leaning forward across my desk as I'm now back in the office, "we carry more than we're meant to. And it feels heavy, doesn't it?"

The junior sitting across from me nods. She's crashing out over the grades, sports, and a very embarrassing breakup. I know that look—drowning while trying to appear fine. It's like I'm staring in a mirror. Her more messy than neat blond ponytail slides over her shoulder as she leans forward while she gives her oversized sleeves of her school hoodie a tug. She's got so many signs of being overwhelmed. "It doesn't mean you're weak," I add softly. "It means you're human. And it's okay to ask for help."

"Who is there to ask? I mean, I thought that's why I came to see you." She sniffles, and I slide a tissue box across my desk.

"Coming here was a great first step, and you're welcome to come any time. Let's start by addressing your schedule. Have you written down everything in one calendar? I call it a brain dump. Get everything off your mind and onto a piece of paper."

"Yeah, I write down my assignments and practices in my planner, but that doesn't seem to help, as it's a lot to look at." She shifts in my armchair, all the while letting one sneaker tap nervously against the metal leg of the desk.

"Let me ask you this?" I slide to the edge of my seat. "Have you scheduled any time for fun things? Maybe a movie with friends. If you learn to block off downtime, that can help give you assurance it will balance."

"No, I don't do anything like that." She straightens a little in the chair, fingers fidgeting with the armrests.

"I think you should try. After you plug everything in for the week, go back and block out at least thirty minutes a day where you know you can do something either fun or relaxing. Then come back tomorrow, and we'll talk some more." I hate to wrap up the conversation so soon, but the bell rings right when I get my last word out. I don't have to ask her to leave, as she gathers her things and says, "Thank you, Mrs. Anton," in the smallest breath.

"You're welcome." My voice is steady, but the moment she's out the door, my smile deflates. I've never faked this job more than I have lately. Do I actually believe any of this advice?

My phone buzzes in the drawer, and my gaze slides down to an unknown number. It's probably a robocall, but there's a chance it's the doctor's office, and I urgently answer it. "Hello."

"Mrs. Anton?" The voice is polite. "This is June, Dr. Tang's nurse. We have your test results."

My stomach drops as I've been impatiently waiting. "Yes," I whisper.

"Well, it looks like we found something. Your thyroid levels are abnormal," she says in an even tone. "We'd like you to come in to discuss treatment options."

"My thyroid." The words tumble around me. "What does that mean?"

"It means your thyroid isn't working properly and could be the reason why you're feeling tired, among other things. Dr. Tang would like to see you back here this week. Do you have time tomorrow?"

"Yeah." I click the mouse on my desk until my computer screen flashes to life, and I check my schedule. There really isn't anything I can move around to another time slot. So much for me carving out fun time like I just told that girl. I'm such a fraud. I'm packed all day every day for the next two weeks. With a heavy sigh, I say, "Why don't you just tell me what time works for Dr. Tang, and I'll call in sick."

"How about first thing in the morning? Eight o'clock."

"I will make it work." I highlight my schedule, marking myself out for sick leave, and then say, "Thank you." I hang up the phone and stare at my computer screen, the words "sick leave" glowing bright, and my throat burns. What if I'm really sick? *It's okay to be scared. Everything works out.* My counselor voice echoes in my head.

I close my eyes, press my palms flat to the desk, and breathe.

One step at a time.

For now, just breathe.

Twenty

BLAKE

The pub buzzes with every seat filled. Celebratory voices rise over the sports highlights on the TVs. The noise doesn't stop me from doing what I came to do. I've been on an adrenaline high for days. Everything I'm doing to start this team has been working out. I take each win and use it as fuel for the next one. "Gentlemen and ladies." I raise my glass to the small circle of potential investors I invited tonight. "Cheers to the future of hockey."

They cheer, some louder than others. To my surprise, Trey Micheal has joined me again, and he reads over contracts spread across the table. I can tell he's very smart by the way he reads every line on every page. After a while, he leans in and says, "You've got charisma, Blake. That is what makes this enticing, but charisma doesn't sell tickets. Have you followed Bill Baker's team much? He has the newest team in the league, and he's got so much money in that team, and they still aren't winning. What are you going to do differently?"

Bill's name twists in my gut, locking my jaw tight. I struggle not to show he's the reason I want this team. I lean back, smirking cool as steel. "Bill's floundering out there in Vermont, because he's in over his head. He's in an undesirable location. Plus, he took guys on his roster who should never have been there. Now he's suffering for it. I'm not Bill, and I won't make his mistakes. I won't be building a team of rookies, and we're in New York, a more attractive location for recruits and fans. There really isn't any comparison."

Trey studies me for a beat and chuckles. "You sure are cocky, but I like it."

The table erupts in more laughter, and I lap it up. My grin slides wide. "To the first puck drop," I declare. "And all the ones after that!"

The table roars, and we click our glasses, chanting, "All the pucks."

Now it's my turn to pivot to a banner draped in a black-and-purple cloth. I quietly stride over to it and remove the cloth, revealing my new team logo and name.

Arctic Force.

It sounds special.

I flash them all my cockiest grin. My pulse kicks higher, adrenaline flooding like I've scored a goal. I should be reveling in this—this is what I fought for. The investors are on board, the arena is locked down, but my eyes keep catching on empty spaces. Involuntarily, I imagine Lacey at the table next to me. Yeah, she would be here with her proud smile, squeezing my hand. For a split second, I can almost hear her voice—*You did it, Blake!*

But she isn't here.

It's just the deafening echo of her absence.

I rub a hand over my face, releasing a forced breath.

I have everything I ever wanted—power, respect, plans in motion for my own AHL team. But what good is it if I can't come home and share it with her? My phone buzzes in my pocket. For one stupid, hopeful second, I think it might be her. I yank it out with one quick movement.

It's Peyton.

He's standing across the room from me, so I'm not sure why he'd text. I open it up and find a photo of my daughter with that Granite Ice player. It's a screenshot of the Granite Ice social media page. They are just standing next to each other by the ice rink in a totally innocent position, but Paisley's eyes are sparking at him.

My jaw tightens.

I can tell by the way Paisley's eyes are locked on him, this isn't a platonic thing. There's no way I'm letting my daughter date one of Bill's hockey players, let alone his stepson.

That can't happen!

She'll also never forgive me if I try to break them up, even if she would listen to me, which she'd never do. It's time I move on to the next phase of my plan.

It's time for me to bring Paisley back and steal Bill's player.

Instead of texting Peyton back, I nod at him and close his text. Then, since I can't help myself, I find Lacey's name. Maybe I'm just too weak, but I can't stop. I've been texting her everyday just to tell her I love her. Sure, I forgot to say that for so many days, but I've made it a mission to never let a day pass from this time forward without declaring my love for her.

> **Lacey, I'm so sorry I never appreciated you enough, but your absence is killing me. Please, forgive me. I love you so much. Nothing else matters if I don't have you.**

Then I press "Send," stuff my phone back in my pocket, and smile back at the people smiling at me. I check my phone every ten minutes, pretending I'm not. Pretending I'm focused. But really, I'm waiting for the three dots. She read it—I know she did. And still, nothing.

It gnaws at me so strongly until I finally give up and sneak out the side door. This celebration means nothing without her. I've played while hurt before, broken bones, torn muscles, but one thing I never did was quit. I hope she knows me well enough to know that. She better be prepared. I won't quit on her.

I swipe my phone awake again.

Still nothing.

My chest burns even hotter. Fine. If she won't answer now, she'll see eventually how hard I'm trying.

Drinks couldn't wrap up soon enough. With still so much to do, I head back to my office, prepared to stay up all night working. The phone stays stubbornly silent. Lacey's absence presses down on me like a weight I can't lift. So, I start on the one thing I have left to do. I make calls to agents to fill out my roster. Hours blur into one another. I reach out to old contacts, former teammates, and scouts. Some laugh, some hesitate, and some jump right into negotiations like they can smell the money I've raised.

And then it happens.

A name pops up on my incoming calls, almost casually, like it isn't the grenade it is: Bill Baker. I lean back in my chair, fighting the smile tugging at my mouth.

Of course I'm accepting this call.

"Bill," I answer in my gruffest voice.

"Blake," he counters with an equally tough voice. "You sent your daughter to destroy my team, and you suck at it."

"What do you want, Bill?" I cut right to the chase. We'll never be friends, and I'm not admitting to anything, even if he's right about me sucking at that, because it backfired when Paisley fell for his stepson.

"I'm not going to have a traitor on my team," Bill goes on. "Noah insists he won't break up with Paisley, so I want them both out of here, and you're all over the news about this Arctic Force team. I'm hearing from scouts you're building your roster. I don't need your daughter hanging around here, and I'm ready to teach Noah a lesson. What do you say, you take them both off my hands?"

My jaw actually drops. Like, cartoon-style, hinge-un-hinged, mouth-on-the-floor kind of drop. Because there's no way this is happening. He's literally dropping them right into my lap, and I'm ready to scoop it all back. It's *too easy.*

Bill Baker is offering up Noah like it's nothing. Like he's handing over a free puppy, not the key to saving my marriage and my daughter. "What's the catch?" I ask, tilting my head, doing my best to sound bored instead of borderline hyper-ventilating.

"No catch. It seems like the right move for both of us." He mirrors my bored sounding tone.

Inside, my heart is doing the full marching band half-time show. "It sounds," I start slowly, as if every word costs money, "like I'm interested in hearing more." I close my laptop and lean forward. "Let's talk," I say, channeling every ounce of calm I don't feel.

"It's just like I said. Noah doesn't fit our roster anymore," he says but stops fast like he's holding back.

"Right," I say, nodding thoughtfully.

"And he insists he wants to stay with Paisley."

"Which is why you're offering him to me out of the goodness of your heart?"

"Don't flatter yourself." He chuckles, low and smug. "You happen to have an asset I could use."

"Asset?" I echo. "What are you talking about?"

"Well, I heard from one of my scouts that you called him, and you snagged a Minnesota player I had my eye on."

"Uh, you're talking about a certain number 32." My eyes narrow, but I keep smiling. "And you think I'm giving him up just like that?"

"Or maybe," he says, "I can keep Noah here and offer him a big raise, and who knows, maybe Paisley can even move in the house here with all of us."

I laugh sharply. "Ha! That will never happen." Silence follows. Neither of us wants to make the next move.

We stay quiet for too long. Then I pick up my pen and start jotting on the notepad. "Fine. Let's say I take Noah off your hands. You get number 32, and it's a fair trade. If you say yes now, I'll even throw your dignity for having to beg back in."

Bill laughs. "Still as cocky as ever."

"Still threatened as ever," I shoot back. My heart is slamming against my rib cage so hard I lean back in the chair to steady myself and cross one boot over the opposite knee.

"You know, I almost miss this."

"Fighting with me?"

"We can wait until we meet on the ice to see who's winning." I smile sweetly, even though no one is here to see it. If this goes the way I think it will, Bill Baker just handed me the one player who'll crush his entire season—and save my marriage.

"All right, Anton," he says with a gruff tone in his voice. "I'll have a contract sent over in the next hour." The line goes dead before I can reply. I set my phone down and my gaze slides back to the wall where I have my Granite Ice Logo target, and in a surprise twist of emotion, my gut sinks. I should be celebrating pulling Bill's stepson and getting my daughter to move back home. It's a huge win.

But instead, all I can think about is calling Lacey.

I so badly want to tell her everything I'm doing to help our family.

I close my eyes, and the memories come uninvited.

All the sudden we are back in high school:

After practice, we sat on the tailgate of my truck, her boots lightly knocking each other, steam rising from her hot chocolate. She'd just broken it off with Bill, and we both knew it was coming. We'd been respectful, not crossing a line while she was dating him, but now that she was single, the tension was unbearable.

"I can't believe you're really going to the NHL," she said. "You'll forget all about this place."

"Not a chance." My voice cracked. All I'd been doing for weeks was trying my hardest to forget about her and the feelings I experienced when I took her to the prom, but they were an unstoppable force. She gazed at me, and the world got dizzy in a heart-thudding kind of way. I didn't plan it and heaven knows I didn't think about it, or I would have chickened out. I just leaned.

"You've got that look again," she said, stopping me before I made it all the way to her lips.

"What look?"

"The one that makes me nervous."

My heart kicked hard. "Then stop looking."

But she didn't.

And I took that as an invitation to lean in the rest of the way to kiss her. My hand trembled, and she reached for it, and it steadied into hers, like we were meant to be like that. She tasted like chocolate and every good thing I didn't know I needed yet.

Since that day, she has ruined me for chocolate. I've never been able to have any without thinking of that moment. Funny how life proves you wrong in the quietest ways. Somewhere between the nights I came home too late and the time we spent eating dinner together on the couch, I stopped chasing her.

It wasn't on purpose.

It was just life.

And now, sitting here with my phone heavy in my hand and her silence louder than any crowd I ever played for, I'd give anything to go back and do it all differently.

I miss her.

Not just the wife.

Not just the mother of my kids.

Her.

The girl who once stared at me like I was her whole world. And I'm so sorry I stopped giving her reasons to look at me that way.

Twenty-One

LACEY

Hashimoto's thyroiditis.

Staring at my Google bar, where I've typed the words, my finger pauses on the entry. Dr. Tang assured me that with medication, it's manageable. In some way, I'm relieved to know there's a reason I've been feeling so exhausted. Even still, my heart thumps in my chest as I prepare myself to see what Google says. I swallow and slowly press enter. The screen flashes, pulling up an entire list of articles. My gaze hasn't quite registered anything when a figure slides into my doorway. I glance up from my desk, expecting a student needing a schedule change.

But to my surprise, it's Paisley!

She's dressed in her normal hue of rebellion—black. Black high-waisted jeans with the knees faintly worn, paired with an oversized charcoal sweater that's at least two sizes too big. Her dark hair falls in uneven waves, hinting it was brushed at some point today. She's exactly the way I'd expect her to look, but the thing that alarms me is her eyes luster in a way I've never seen them shine.

I recognize the emotion right away.

She's clearly in love.

Blinking, I do a double take but there's no mistaking her expression. Quickly, I minimize my internet browser, as I don't want her to worry about me. I brace myself and stand with my arms wide for a hug. "Hey, honey! I didn't know you were back in town."

She leans in to my embrace and then drops into the chair across from me. "I want to tell you before you freak out," she blurts. "I'm dating someone, and I'm moving back home."

"Congratulations. Honey, I can't wait to hear everything about him." I have to stop to catch my breath. The words knock the air from my chest. Blake had told me she was seeing Bill's stepson, but this is the first she's come to me about it. I also get hung up on something else she said, and I force my counselor's calm into my voice. "Moving back where? Your apartment?"

Her smile widens into a dreamy wistful slant. "No, *home* home. I'm not sure if you heard, but Dad was able to recruit Noah, my boyfriend, for his team. It caused a rift between him and his stepdad, and he got kicked out and is basically homeless, with no paycheck, until he starts practice for Arctic Force, but that won't be for a while. We are both here, and he needs a place to stay for a while. We aren't going to live together." She pauses as red streaks up her neck, and her fingers find the hem of her sweater. Completely avoiding my gaze, she adds, "I thought he could crash at my place while I stay at home. You know, just until he gets on his feet and finds a place of his own."

My heart ticks up a notch. She is unaware I'm not living at home, and I'm not ready to have that conversation. Not here or before I talk to Blake. Sure, I had all summer, but telling the kids I've moved out is so final, and I never wanted this to be final. I just haven't healed the way I had expected, which honestly makes sense. I can't undo decades of neglect in a few months, but I'm making progress with my new meds I literally started today. Who knows what those can do for me? I'm not ready to give up on my marriage yet...

My brain is swirling with something else. There's something about that name, *Noah,* that sticks in my throat, but I don't recall him. "I'm confused. So, why would your boyfriend get kicked out of his house for getting a new job?"

"Oh, you missed that part." She flicks her hand forward. "Sorry, I figured Dad told you, but Noah is Bill Baker's step-son. Bill doesn't want me dating him. Well, neither did Dad, but Dad's a lot less upset about it now that he's off Bill's team..." Her voice trails off as her gaze finally connects to mine.

My stomach twists.

It's like before I was seeing in black and white, and now my vision explodes with color. It's too many layers, too many tangled loyalties. Add in the look of unguarded love in her eyes, it's enough to rip my heart into two—even as a profes-sional counselor! I have no idea how to navigate this situation. Somehow, I manage a weak smile. "Wow. That's big news."

Her eyes glimmer bright when she gushes, "It's good news, Mom. Right? You'll love Noah. Since he plays hockey, he'll fit right in with the family. He's honestly just like Dad."

A knot wedges in my throat, cinching my airway tighter, and I grip the edge of the desk so hard my knuckles ache.

Because I don't know how to tell her the truth.

She's walking into the middle of a mess she doesn't under-stand. Her heart is tying itself to a rivalry older than she is. That every step closer to her boyfriend pulls her deeper into the storm Blake is creating. And most of all, I don't know how to tell her I no longer live at home, because I was tired of always being last to hockey. That's certainly not the life I want for her. Yet, I know as much as I'm dying inside to warn her, she won't hear it from me. She has to make her own mistakes. I force my counselor smile and pray it hides the panic twisting inside me. "That's a lot to take in, but I'm glad you told me."

She beams and leans over with her arms outstretched to hug me again. I give her a playful side-eye. Paisley isn't exactly the outwardly affectionate type. The fact she's offering a second hug in five minutes is off character for her. Regardless, I'm going to soak it up, and I squeeze her back and swallow, hoping the knot in my throat releases.

No such chance.

As I hug her back, I inhale her clean scent, wishing so hard life didn't have to be so complicated. For all the first loves she could have picked, she picked the exact wrong one. I so miss the days when I could sweep her into my lap, and tell her, "Mommy says no." Those days are long gone. My throat wrings even tighter, and a cold sweat breaks out on my palms.

Noah will change her. Sure, on the outside, she's glowing, but she has no idea about how bad it hurts to be in love with a man who only loves a sport. Nor does she understand about the war between Bill and Blake. She thinks it's purely a hockey rivalry. I never told her about my high school boyfriend. And now these men have pulled my daughter straight into their battlefield. "Well, I'm heading out to meet Noah for lunch." She pulls away from me and slides her foot to the door as if she can't get away fast enough. "Noah's at my place now, making tacos, but I wanted to give you a heads-up that I'll be home tonight for dinner. I was hoping I could invite Noah. He's so excited to meet you. Maybe we could all go out to dinner if Dad can get off work?"

"Tonight?" I blow out a breath. "Uh, sure. That should be fine."

"Perfect." She spins on her heel, heading out the door while throwing her hand up in a wave. "I'll see you after school!"

"Yep." I wave and wait until the hall is quiet again. Then I pull out my phone and dial Blake.

"Lacey." His voice is softer than I've heard it in years, causing me to curl my hand into a fist. Why does it feel like I'm fighting my past? I would have loved to hear this affection in his tone even a year ago, but now it just upsets me.

"Hey," I manage quietly. "Paisley just left my office. She filled me in on what's going on with your trade, Noah. I guess she wants to let him live at her place, and she wants to stay at home."

"Yeah, I had to do what I had to do. There's no way I want her hanging around Bill," he's quick to reply, and if I didn't know better, I'd say desperation flows in his tone.

"I get that." I curl my fingers even tighter, pooling all my strength as I proceed with slower words. "But she doesn't know I've moved out. I don't want to start a bunch of drama with her, not in front of her new boyfriend, anyway. I'll probably come back home tonight. Just so she doesn't suspect anything. I don't know. I can accidentally fall asleep on the couch downstairs, or something, so it's not weird. Is that okay?"

"Of course. You don't ever have to ask. It's your *home*." His voice cracks on the word home.

I exhale. This clearly isn't solving my issues. If anything, it's a step back, but it will buy me some time before I need to explain to the kids what's been going on, because I still don't know how to explain it, as I don't know myself. I have a diagnosis, but nothing else.

"I miss you." I can almost see the deep lines in his brow as he goes on, "I miss *us, and I'm so glad you are coming back.*"

A beat. Then another.

The words haunt. A hand presses to an old bruise that desperately wants to heal, except it can't be left alone long enough. I hate hearing him being sweet makes me hurt, but I can't deny that there's some bitterness. I said those words too. For years, I begged and said I missed him, but he didn't hear me because he was always rushing out the door to another game or to meet another gym member. Heat blooms behind my eye. I hold on to every last tear begging to fall. Before he gets lost in the wrong idea, I add a soft, "I'm not coming home for *us*, Blake."

Before he can reply, I end the call while my chest explodes, and I scamper toward my open door and close it, all the while my chest hiccups with suppressed emotions. As soon as the door is closed, I slam my back against it and break into sobs. This isn't how I planned my life to go, and now poor Paisley is repeating my mistakes.

Twenty-Two

Blake

Lacey's blue Toyota pulls up in the driveway, and I start pacing in the foyer. Paisley is still at her apartment with that Miller boy, so it's just us in the house, and my pulse goes full overtime—no whistles, no mercy.

Gracefully, Lacey gets out of her car and moves around to the trunk. With so many emotions swirling in my head, I can't hear anything. It's all static and white noise, and I give up trying to act casual and fly through the front door without shoes to help her with her luggage. Forget that it's just a degree above freezing. I was born for the cold. For a split second, it feels like I'm seventeen again.

A soft, oversized baby blue sweater clings to her in all the best ways. Her ivory creased linen pants are wrinkled at the knees from working all day, and she has flat white sneakers on. A canvas tote digs into her shoulder, and it's half-unzipped with the strap tangled at the top.

She spots me, and her whole face stills. I wait for a smile, the one that always used to greet me when I came home, but her shoulders draw in, and she dips her chin as if avoiding my gaze while she presses her lips together. I stop in front of the open trunk, not sure of how I should greet her. It feels so completely unnatural not to wrap my arms around her and hug her. I know she doesn't want it, which fractures my heart at the seams. What I wouldn't do to go back in time, back to the days when she'd run into my arms...After a lonely beat, I motion forward to the open trunk. "Can I grab your bags?"

Instead of replying, she steps forward and wraps her hand around the handle to the suitcase closest to her and tugs on it until it's removed, and she sets it on the driveway next to her. "I'm not sure what all I will bring in. I checked out of my Airbnb. Figured I might as well save the money, so I have everything, but I might not need it all. Maybe just that white one too." She nods toward the biggest one, and I don't waste a second grabbing it for her.

I stay behind her as she walks up our walkway, through the front door, and her gaze automatically pulls to the kitchen and then upstairs. "Paisley is still at her place," I say. "With Noah."

"Oh." Lacey's lips bend into a cautious smile. "I guess that's good for her."

"Why don't you relax, and I'll take your bags upstairs—" I interrupt myself by throwing my hands up in a stop gesture and insert, "It's best you take the bedroom. I'll sleep in my office. I've been going to the gym so early these days, Paisley won't even notice."

"Okay." She takes a couple of steps into the kitchen, where I don't miss her loud exhale. Then I turn on my heel and take the steps two at a time to get her bags stowed. When I return, I find her sitting at the table, just looking around like she's trying to remember things.

The silence pulsates.

Moisture gathers at the base of my spine. It's one of those moments where I can feel the weight in my chest. Like it has the power to either set us up for a positive encounter, or one wrong word and I'm headed straight to the penalty box. I don't want to pressure her. As much as I want to tell her how much I still love her, my heart knows she won't sit here and listen to that. What I want more than anything is to just talk to her, like we used to. We used to laugh for hours. The mere memory makes my fingers curl into a tight fist. My heart tells me if I'm going to get that back, I can't pressure her. It's better to try to be a friend. Ease the tension, so she's comfortable here. The only way I know how to do that is to try to be funny, but that's a risk because she's clearly not laughing at me much these days. I clear my throat, leaning back against the fridge. "So, do I look older?"

She raises a brow at me. "You mean compared to when you had a mullet in high school?"

"That wasn't a mullet." I portray mock shock by dropping my jaw open. "That was my flow. It's a hockey hair thing, and it's totally different. You, of all people, should know that, as all the boys had it too."

"The boys had long hair at times, but you..." she groans. "You used more hair spray than I did."

"This is unbelievable." I scrub a hand down my face, and tease, "I come in here ready to pour my heart out, and you're roasting my hair choice from twenty-five years ago."

She grows a small grin, sending a ping of hope to my heart. "Someone has to keep your ego in check."

Sure, it's an insult, but it feels like how we used to flirt, and it lands so perfectly in my chest, inflating that ego she just insulted. I take a risk. "You're the only one who ever could."

She looks away, focusing her gaze out the window. After a beat of silence, she says, "Did you have dinner plans?"

"I didn't. I, ah, stocked the fridge with some of your favorite things. That creamer you like for your coffee, and cream cheese and bagels for the morning. There's salmon and steak. I could throw some on the grill."

Propping both elbows on the table, she leans forward. "Well, Paisley asked if we could meet her for dinner, so we can meet her...*boyfriend*." She hesitates on that last word, and it rings in my head like a gong. Paisley told me all about Noah, but I'll never get used to hearing my baby girl has a boyfriend. Wasn't she like three-years-old only yesterday? Lacey tacks on, "Would it be okay if we go together, and just for tonight put everything about us aside? For her sake."

It's my turn to blink. For months I've been on pins and needles, waiting for the final buzzer on our marriage, but she just reset the clock. I can work with this! "I would love to." I don't even pretend to downplay how much it means to me that she's extending this lifeline. I quickly survey my gym sweats, and say, "I'll change into something clean. Did you want to reach out to her and see if she has a place in mind, or I can make a reservation too."

"I'll text her." Lacey drops her gaze to her phone on the table and starts typing. I don't wait for her to say anything else. I can't stop smirking as I dart up the stairs. It's stupid, I know. I'm a grown man and a father of four. Here I am blushing like a teenager who just got asked on a first date, and it's not even a date. But the thing is, at least while Paisley is in the house, Lacey won't be able to avoid me, which means,

I'll finally have the chance I need to show her I'm ready to change.

No, not ready. I am changed—forever.

Seeing her walk out that door gutted me in a way I'll never get over and never forget. I will do anything, as long as it means I don't have to repeat that day. She may think she's only here for a day or two, but little does she know, I have big plans.

The tightening that's deep in my gut lightens.

I know she is here for Paisley and not for me, but I have to believe there's hope.

Twenty-Three

Lacey

Despite being back under the same roof as Blake, my mind feels a clarity I don't remember having in a long time. The bone-deep fatigue is finally easing. The only thing that has changed is the meds I've been taking. It's too early to say they are working, but it seems like I'm able to focus better. I also didn't gag at the thought of having to eat dinner next to Blake.

That has to mean something, even if I don't know what.

I'm actually feeling so calm, I'm fine when he offers to drive us both over there. I was so shocked at my own reply, we both dropped our jaws and stared at each other as if we were waiting for a correction, but for real, I'm fine riding together. It makes sense as we are leaving and going to the same place.

Now we ride in his car like nothing has changed between us. The even more shocking thing is Blake made an effort to look nice, as he left his gym rat clothes at home. I honestly didn't think he had nice clothes that fit him anymore but somehow, he managed to pull out a dark blazer and pressed shirt. I can't remember the last time he wore a shirt without a sweat ring around his neck. And the way his face lit up when I suggested going out? Heaven help me, my knees actually went weak.

It was exactly the kind of attention I've been craving for years. Being desired by your husband, even if it's just sharing a meal together. When we pull into the parking lot, Blake rushes out, seemingly to open the door for me. I open it before he can, because I don't need him to think he can win my love by being chivalrous for a measly day. I will give it to him. He's trying, but one dinner isn't erasing years of neglect.

The restaurant Paisley picked is comfortable in that homey way. Relief poured through me; nobody insisted on going to a sport's restaurant. My days competing with TV screens are officially over. Instead of the high-top table Blake normally autopilot requests, the place is filled with only booths.

As soon as Paisley catches sight of us, she waves us over, as if we weren't already heading her way. I walk fast, staying more than a step in front of Blake to ensure I'm out of his reach.

I don't need him to accidentally place his hand on my back. He'd more than likely claim it as an old habit, but I don't put it past him one bit to take advantage of this time to try to lure me back to him.

As soon as we are in earshot, Paisley's hands flutter in front of her like they are fueling her words. "Noah, this is my dad, Blake, and my mom, Lacey. Obviously, this is *Noah*." She proclaims his name like we've been waiting for him all our lives, making me chuckle.

Noah leans across the table and extends his hand, mercilessly aiming his deep cheek dimple my way. I see it immediately. My dear sweet, naïve daughter never had a chance with that dimple. "Nice to meet you both." He shakes my hand first, and I hold my breath, as this hits me a lot harder than I had planned.

Then he turns to Blake, who sparks a flicker of recognition from the center of his eyes. Noah's smile falters for a beat, as one would expect from a man meeting his girlfriend's father, who is also his new boss. I was so focused on Noah's dimple, I missed pulling out my chair, and Blake slides in front of me, beating me to it. I flash him with a useless smile and take my seat. Everyone else follows my cue. I don't miss Blake's smile is all teeth when he hooks his gaze on Noah and gets right to business, "So, I saw you returned your contract. You are officially on Arctic Force. You did the right thing."

Noah chuckles nervously. "Thank you, sir. It's an honor to play for your team. I'm a huge fan of yours."

Blake leans back, crossing his arms into his "casual" posture, which is about as natural as a bear on a barstool. "And by fan, what do you know about me?"

I kick him under the table. This isn't the time to pump his ego, but he doesn't wince. His eyes stay lasered on Noah.

"You have a great record," Noah says quickly as he slides his gaze to Paisley, as if it hurts to look at Blake. "I've watched some of your old footage, and you have impressive stickhandling."

Blake grunts, which, in his language can easily translate into a *"You may continue to exist sitting next to my daughter for now."*

"This is such a treat to get together this evening." I swoop in with the best peacekeeping grin I can manage. "Noah, how about you share all the fun stuff? How did you and Paisley meet?"

Paisley's face lights up like something I've never seen, and she rushes to say, "Officially I first saw him at the arena, but we didn't meet until the gala." She glances at him, her cheeks flushed with red. "He helped me after I fell on the floor." She removes the paper ring from her silverware, her hands clearly trembling. She really likes this boy. Maybe even worse.

Noah places his hand on hers. "She was literally trapped because of all the people crowding in." He shakes his head. "I'm still flabbergasted by the whole incident."

Paisley smiles at him, then glances at her hand, her cheeks turning even a brighter shade of red. "It was bad, but I guess it worked out, because I doubt you would have talked to me otherwise." Paisley clears her throat, reaches for her water glass, and takes a sip.

Blake follows her lead and picks up his water glass, muttering, "I'm sure that's all he wanted to do was talk."

I shoot him a warning look, but Paisley groans. "Dad!"

Noah, to his credit, takes it in stride, only hiking one eyebrow. "If it helps, sir, I didn't know anything about Bill and your conflict until long after we started hanging out. Bill and my mom just got married, and he really didn't tell me a whole lot about that stuff."

Blake doesn't twitch a lip to respond, and the waiter returns, saving us all from having to discuss all the messy stuff. As the waiter lists the specials, I'm thinking about how strange it is, sitting next to the man I'm separated from—still technically married to—trying to look like we haven't been sleeping in separate houses for weeks.

The waiter places his pen at a sharp angle over his notepad. "Is everyone ready to order?"

Paisley glances at Noah. "We are ready." Paisley looks at me. "But they just arrived and might need a minute—"

"We're ready." Blake waves his hand to insert his comment and goes on to order for me. "She'll have the shrimp scampi with a side salad, and I'll have the same."

The waiter looks at me as if to confirm, and I nod. "That sounds perfect." Because it does. Blake always knows what I like. His eyes lock on me when he hands the menus back to the waiter. I barely hear what Noah and Paisley order. As soon as the waiter walks away, Blake's gaze locks on Noah again. "Just so you know, dating my daughter doesn't mean more ice time."

"Blake," I hiss and stomp on his foot.

Noah only smiles. "Understood, sir. I'll earn it."

Paisley rolls her eyes, but she's still smiling.

"Can we talk about something other than hockey?" I say.

"Oh sure." Blake's transition is smooth, like he was waiting to bring something up. "So, I found Paul's pet snake the other day."

My head jolts back, as I'm instantly lost. "What pet snake?"

"Don't you remember Scales? Paul brought him home from school when he was back in fourth grade."

"The one I was freaked out by and didn't want to be left home alone with, so you got rid of it." I tip my head to the side, as there's only one snake I ever remember coming into the house. He was gone within two hours, because I insisted I couldn't live with it. "Didn't you take it out in the country and let it go?"

"Ah." His eyes move side to side. "I forgot I did that."

My brows bend down. "How can you forget?"

"Ah, maybe I might have a confession." His eyelids drop, hooding his eyes as he continues, "I said I released him into the country, because Paul actually left the lid off his cage, and Scales got out. I knew if you found out he was slithering around the house, you'd move out."

"What!" My T is extra sharp. "So, he's still alive and living in our house for this whole time?"

"No." Blake holds up a finger. "I can confirm by the skeleton I found in the basement; he is indeed dead."

My hand flies to my chest. I do my best to steady my heart rate, while my mind races over all the years I lived in that house with no idea a snake was roaming around. "Are you trying to kill me?"

"No." A laugh cracks out of him. "I just forgot that you didn't know we never found him."

"Wow, that's quite an update." I take a moment to chew on the inside of my cheek before asking, "Anything else you need to update me on?"

"Nope. Not like that anyway." He drops his tone. "But I am glad to have Paisley back home again." His expression softens as his gaze shifts back to her.

The waiter returns and slides our plates neatly onto the table. The smell of garlic and butter fills the air. Noah beams as he straightens his napkin on his lap. "That looks amazing."

Paisley grins back. "Yeah, glad I went with the pasta."

Happy to have something to focus on other than a dead snake in my house, I stab at my shrimp with frantic energy. Seriously, it's stunts like these that make Blake a challenge to love.

"So," Blake interjects after taking a polite-sized bite of his shrimp. "Noah, you must have grown up playing hockey."

He twirls his pasta around his fork, keeping his gaze focused. "Pretty much. My mom was single and ran a diner with my grandma. When I wasn't there or at school, I was playing hockey.

Blake doesn't even look up as he's shoveling fork after fork into his mouth. "Do you mean that Mapleton truck stop diner off the interstate?"

Noah also keeps his gaze down. "Yeah. It's pretty humble."

Blake hums out a groan, and I reach for my water, smiling sweetly. "Ignore him, Noah. He gets territorial about his food and his daughter."

Noah nods, and offers, "Noted."

A beat of silence follows, filled only by the clinking of silverware, where Paisley valiantly attempts to change the subject. "So, Noah's moved into my apartment, and he's mostly settled."

"Oh?" Blake says, instantly alert. "You're taking over the rent, right?"

"Yes," Noah says. "I might get a roommate to help out. One of the other players from the team or something."

"A roommate is fine," Blake adds, like he owns the building, instead of simply having his name on the lease. "But no co-ed sleepovers."

Noah chokes and rushes out, "Yeah, no sleepovers. It will be just me and my PlayStation."

That gets a laugh out of me, and even Blake cracks a reluctant smile. Noah must be building confidence because he slides his hand over Paisley's again, leaving his affection on the table for us all to see. An earlier version of myself might not appreciate how bold he is about that, but having spent years begging my husband for affection, public hand-holding is a win in my book.

Paisley exhales and takes a second to look at me and then Blake before glancing over at Noah. "See? Everyone's fine with everything."

We're all nodding and smiling like a sitcom family when the waiter appears again, topping off our glasses. "Does anyone need anything else?"

"Maybe a dessert menu?" I ask politely.

Blake shoots me a teasing look. He knows how much I love dessert because it's usually a form of chocolate. I catch the corner of his mouth twitch before he deadpans back on Noah. "So, how do you feel about curfews?"

The waiter's eyes spring wide open, and he slips quietly away as Noah freezes for a solid ten seconds before he says, "Ah, love them."

Paisley drops her fork with a *clink.* "Dad! I'm eighteen."

Laughter bubbles up my throat because I remember Blake never getting me home on time. I certainly won't bring that up now. Those extra stolen minutes made the best memories.

The waiter returns with the dessert menu, peering right at me. "Anyone else saving room for dessert?"

"Actually, I changed my mind." My gaze floats back to Noah, his cheeks still glowing a nice rose color. He's been a great sport, and I don't think I need to put him through another round of food and interrogations. "I enjoyed my shrimp so much, I cleaned my plate, and I'm actually full."

Blake clears his throat and pushes his water glass forward, murmuring to the waiter, "You can bring the check, please."

Noah immediately sits up straighter. "Oh, no, sir, please—let me—"

Blake waves him off. "Nah, save your money."

The waiter slides the little black folder onto the table. Blake snatches it up before Noah can blink and pulls out his wallet with dramatic flair.

"Wow," I say, tilting my head.

"Don't start," he warns, but he's smiling when he says it.

Noah reaches for the check again. "At least let me cover the tip."

Blake shakes his head. "You'll have plenty of chances to pay me back on the ice."

There's a collective groan, with mine being the loudest of all, but even I'm grinning as we stand to leave. Paisley hooks her arm through Noah's and beams like everything in her world is exactly as it should be. "That wasn't so bad, right?" she says as we walk toward the door.

I glance at Blake, who's glaring at Noah holding Paisley's arm.

"No, sweetheart," I tell her. "Not bad at all."

"Hey, no one goes home yet," Blake calls out as we inch toward the exit. "First Noah and I have to settle something—"

"Dad." Paisley plants her feet, her stance wide, hands on her hips. "What are you doing?"

He grins cocky and nods for us to walk outside.

"Where are we going?" I take a step out as my curiosity is piqued.

"Noah and I are going to do some bonding." He nods down the block and I squint, checking all the little stores, passing them over. Nothing makes sense until I spot the neon sign at the end of the block. An old arcade we used to take the kids to. We've held more than a few birthday parties there over the years. Now I know what he's up to. "You never grow up, do you, Blake?" I tease as we all start strolling toward the sign.

"This doesn't have anything to do with maturity." Blake's chest puffs up the way it always does when he's about to do something competitive. He reaches forward and opens the door, allowing us all to walk through first.

Neon-buzzing lights are everywhere. It's loud, chaotic, absolutely not where I'd prefer to spend my Friday night, but that's the thing about being married to Blake. Somehow, he's always been good at getting me out of my comfort zone. Blake goes right to the ticket dispenser, pays for four cards, and hands them out to us while grinning like he's got a secret. "Whoever earns the most tickets, wins. Winner gets to pick what happens next," he says.

I arch an eyebrow. "Like what? You have to finally admit I was right about the Christmas lights incident of 2015?"

"That wasn't a fire!" he blurts back. "There was no need for the fire department to be called either. They confirmed it was just the line sparking. It was a faulty outlet. Something completely out of my control."

Paisley and I pinch back a giggle to save his pride.

"And no, I will never admit to anything else, but I know you wanted dessert." He pins a challenging look at me. "I could see it in your eyes. So, I was thinking more along the lines of who calls where we pick up dessert on the way back to the house."

"Same thing." I raise a coy shoulder in his direction.

Paisley and Noah stride off toward the Skee-Ball lanes. Noah's sleeves are pushed up, and he's got a half-smile tugging at the corner of his mouth.

I don't even have to ask what Blake wants to play. We move in unison to the air hockey table. We've spent so many nights here with the kids, it's pure muscle memory. I slide a red mallet from the rack; he already has the blue one spinning in his palm. My heart also retains muscle memory. One that strains from all the wonderful nights we spent here with the kids. In truth, I love seeing this side of him again, taking time for his wife and family. I don't get my hopes up though. I anticipate this to be short-lived.

He grins, the same cocky tilt he's had since forever. "Ready to lose?"

Not waiting for my reply, he releases the puck, and the familiar *clack-clack-clack* fills the space between us. He never does anything halfway and lunges like the fate of the world relies on every single shot. It's no surprise he's first to score, and he throws his arms up and lets out a ridiculous whoop that turns a few heads.

"Oh, come on." I'm laughing at how the puck shot off the side and somehow angled right into my goal. "That didn't even touch your mallet."

He leans on the table as he reaches for the puck out of my goal. "Pure skill."

I narrow my eyes, readying the puck again. "Uh-huh. Keep telling yourself that." I notice Noah and Paisley as they float from machine to machine, winning tickets together, more as a supportive team. They are not competitive like Blake and me. We've always been like this. I have to admit it's when we've always had the most fun. "Fine," I tell him as he flicks the puck back into play. "We are going for two out of three. It's a mini competition between us. Outside of your challenge."

He leans over the table, his voice dropping enough to make my pulse stutter. "I will stay here all night if it means I get to look at you."

Mustering all my frustration—at least Blake is good for something—I will it to flow through my arm, into my hand, and to the mallet, the stress exploding out, making me feel lighter than I've felt in years. It feels good to hurl pucks at Blake. I keep my gaze low as we spar for a few minutes. Then the unthinkable happens. I score a goal off the left side. I follow his cocky lead, raising my arms up in victory and cheer.

Unfazed, he smiles back at me, waving his paddle. "My mallet was sticky."

"Right." I keep a straight face but giggle. "That's what people say when they lose."

"All right, try again." He resets the puck, and I position myself perfectly behind my goal. The air thickens, and our chuckles fade. Everything feels like it's in slow motion as we spar. My reflexes are better than they've ever been. Maybe it's a side effect of the medication, but I block everything he sends my way. When I see my chance, I send the puck straight down the center, slamming it into the goal. I throw my hand up again. Instead of grumbling, Blake laughs.

Paisley and Noah stop and peer at us from the Pac-Man machine. Just to rub it in a little, I jump up and down and point at Blake with a teasing smile. "I won. You lost."

He's all smiles, but there's a reason why I never get cocky. I'm a klutz. Reveling in my win, I trip over my own foot and stumble forward. Forever with fast reflexes, Blake sees what's happening and does one of his super lunges. His hands catch my waist, preventing me from falling all the way to the concrete floor, and now I'm suspended in his arms.

And then—*nothing moves.*

His hand presses against my fabric coat. Every nerve in my body fires, remembering him. The way we used to fit together perfectly without trying. He waits a beat while I steady myself, and then he slowly releases me as he clears his throat.

Paisley's first to speak. "Are you okay, Mom?"

"I'm fine." I smooth my coat as I study the wall, seeing how close I was to smacking my head against it. "I'll probably sit the rest of the night out, basking in my victory."

Blake snorts and shakes his head as his gaze finds Noah. "Well, I think it's your turn to lose at air hockey. What do you say?"

Noah steps forward with nervous eyes, taking my spot in front of the table. "Sure."

Twenty-Four

BLAKE

"First to three?" Noah leans one hand on the table as he effortlessly tosses the mallet over and over like a big showoff.

"Sure." I swipe my card and wait for the table to turn on. "Don't go easy on me just because I sign your checks."

He snickers, rolling his neck in a circle before hooking his gaze sharply on mine. "Wouldn't dream of it, sir."

The air starts, Noah hits the puck on the face-off first and takes an easy shot. I let him do that, so he doesn't embarrass himself. Of course I block it and send it back skimming along

his edge, and *bam*! It slides right in his goal. "One-nothing,"
I say, trying hard not to celebrate too much.

Noah exhales loudly as he resets the puck. "Beginner's
luck."

"Ha! I've been playing this game since before you were
born. I'm far from a beginner."

He sends the puck back to me—harder this time. I guess
he figured out I'm not going easy on him. I slam it back with
so much force, the whole table shakes. We both lean in, eyes
tracing the puck as we spar, until Noah gets lucky with a
clean shot through the center, and it lands in my goal. I pretty
much let him have that too. Just to give him some hope. I
wait for him to rejoice, but he just nods and updates the score.
"One-one."

"Oh, well, I guess I'll have to start trying." The polite tension that's been here all night starts to melt, and I chirp, "You
always this slow? I might have to give you back to Bill."

Noah chuckles loudly this time, throwing his head back.
"Only when I'm letting my boss win."

I bark out laughter before I can stop myself. I didn't expect him to go there, not with him standing next to my
daughter. Before I know it, the next shot slips right past him.
"Two-one," Noah says with a calm voice, but I sense his confidence is cracking.

He resets the puck, and Paisley snickers behind me as she
scoots closer to Noah. It's not lost on me that this is the first

time I've ever seen her do that. She was never a daddy's girl, but she's always cheered for me in everything I've done. My heart squeezes seeing her standing next to someone who isn't me. I guess that's life. It had to happen sometime. I turn to my left. Lacey's standing behind me, where she always used to stand, like she's still on my team. That sends a spark right to my chest, raising my heart like it had been unmoored. I know better than to think her standing next to me is anything other than a convenience so she can watch the game, but it does something to me. I'm not fighting against Noah for fun. I'm fighting for my wife. I can't let her see me lose at a cheesy game like air hockey. My nostrils flare. I track the puck and reach across the table, using the full length of my arm, and slam it with every ounce of force I have. In no time, it ricochets off the side and lands in Noah's goal. I'm cocky when I call it, "Three-one, me."

Noah shakes his head, laughing, as he racks his mallet and moves back to Paisley's side. He's all smiles when he says, "I'll take a rematch on the ice. I'm going to need to see how you skate. No canes allowed."

We all laugh at that, but my attention is on Lacey. She smiles at me. I so badly wish I knew what she's thinking. My heart balloons with joy being near her like this. I rack my mallet and follow them as they start heading toward the exit. No one mentions tallying our tickets to see who won, and I actually don't care either. I'm the last guy out of the door, but I don't feel last tonight. Not with Lacey smiling at me. Tonight, I won.

"Okay." Lacey sighs between chuckles as we climb into my car after saying goodnight to Paisley and Noah. Those two young kids are off to see a late movie, and we're heading back home. "I still can't believe you won against Noah. I think he let you."

"He didn't let me." I'm half offended she'd even say such a thing out loud. I played in the NHL after all. Noah's a good player, but he's not NHL material. Not yet anyway. Maybe after he trains with me a little... I shake my head, mocking shock. "How dare you even suggest that. Did you see the fear in his eyes?"

"Uh-huh." She barely hides a smile. "I'm pretty sure he was trying to get on your good side."

I start the engine and pause, staring at her, soaking up the way Lacey's teasing me. The spark in her eyes hints that she's enjoying herself too. She leans back against the seat, staring out the front window as I shift into gear and drive off.

"You know," she says softly, "it was fun to go back to the arcade. We haven't been there in years. It's funny how the boys grew out of that stage, and I never noticed. Remember when that was a regular Friday night thing? They'd beg for ten dollars. We always pretended like we didn't want to go, but it was always a lot of fun for the whole family..." Her voice trails off, and she pauses before she tacks on something in a whisper, but I catch it. "They had no idea we were falling apart."

I'm quick to catch the glistening in her eyes which just a second ago were happy. My heart was so full a moment ago, now it pulses and folds in on itself. "The ironic thing is," I say, my voice quiet to match her somberness, "it didn't feel like we were falling apart. Not back then. I guess I missed it." Her eyes catch mine when I stop for the red light, and I add, "It didn't feel like we were falling apart tonight either. I had fun."

She blinks, resetting the glistening of her eyes. "I had fun too."

"Maybe that's what we forgot to do." I set my gaze back on the light as it turns green, and I press the gas down again. "Somewhere along the way, we got too serious."

After I make it down another block, her soft whisper echoes in my ear, "Maybe..."

We don't say much after that. Actually, we don't say anything at all. I drive home without so much as even the radio playing. I could turn it on, but then I wouldn't be able to hear the faintest sound of her breathing next to me. It's been so long since I've had that privilege. I don't know when us sitting next to each other like this will happen again, and I can't bear to take it for granted. When I pull into our driveway, she lets out a rare, contented sigh, like she's glad to be home. I close my eyes, pretending she's happy to be home *with me.*

It's after ten, and Paisley hasn't returned from the theater, and it has me a little on edge. Here I am wide awake, lying on the couch in the living room, staring at the ceiling with my mind reeling. I'd never have thought returning to the arcade we used to take the kids to would stir many memories, but I'd forgotten how far we'd come.

Time went too fast.

Lacey and I were stuck in parent mode for so long. Her more than me, as I worked relentless hours to pay for it all. I'd never say it wasn't worth it because my kids are my world, but what I wouldn't give to go back and relive some of those memories again. I grab my phone, my thumb hovers over the screen. Screw it. I've already lost too many years. My chest burns as I type:

I had such a great time tonight.

I stare at the screen, waiting. My heart pounds when her reply lights up.

It was fun to see Paisley so happy. Noah seems like a nice guy too.

I agree, but I also had fun with you. I miss that so much. I love you.

There's a pause long enough for me to wonder if I've pushed too far.

It was nice.

My chest aches. I want to say more. I know she's struggling, and I hate to push it. Instead, I sink deeper into my pillow and drift off to sleep.

"Dad?" Paisley's voice calls from the door, and I glance up. Her eyebrows draw together. "It's almost midnight. What are you doing down here?"

"I can't sleep with you out on a date." I'm quick to sit up and look at my phone like I wasn't sleeping down here. "I had to make sure Noah brought you home at a decent time, and he behaved like a gentleman."

"Noah's fine." She crosses her arms, studying me in a way that makes me feel like *I'm* the teenager now. "This is about Mom, isn't it?"

"What do you mean?" My throat tightens. "What do you know about Mom?"

"She's been acting weird lately. I honestly can't handle the details, but I know she's upstairs and you're down here." She pauses and gives me a dramatic glare. "Stop screwing around and fix it."

I chuckle, shaking my head. "You think it's that easy?"

She shrugs, smirking. "I've never known you to ever give up on anything."

Smarty-pants.

But she's not wrong.

"I have no idea what you're talking about," I blurt out, not wanting to admit anything to Paisley.

"Sure." She rolls her eyes and turns to go upstairs, calling back, "Night, Dad!"

I stare down the hall, wishing that fixing my marriage was as simple as Paisley made it sound.

Twenty-Five

Lacey

Soft footsteps pad down the hall before Paisley's voice carries through the cracked door of my bedroom. "Mom?"

I shift upright against the headboard and open my eyes from the light sleep I was in. "Hey, how did your date go?"

"We saw a thriller, which wasn't my favorite, but it was nice to have that time together." She hesitates. Something else is on her mind, because her eyes keep shifting around the room.

"Good," I say softly, patting the mattress beside me. "Do you want to talk about it or Noah?"

She pads into the room and slides next to me. "There's not a lot to say about that. Noah's been great. I feel lucky to have him." Then her voice drops a notch. "But this isn't about him. Um, why's Dad downstairs?"

My heart stutters. "What do you mean?"

She gives me a look that says she sees more than I want her to. "He's on the couch, and it's clear he's sleeping down there, because he has his favorite pillow. What happened? This can't be about his socks again, because I saw everything was in the hamper."

"It's nothing." I swallow hard, forcing a tight smile. "He's down there because he likes to scroll hockey highlights on his phone, and the light bothers me. He'll be up when he's ready to sleep."

"Right." Her feathered brow arches. "So, how long are we going to pretend I can't feel the tension between you two?"

My breath comes out betrayingly shaky. "Paisley..."

She shakes her head, her voice careful but not unkind. "You don't have to tell me everything. I get Dad can be annoying. But something's off." Her eyes soften. "Just go talk to him. It will be fine. You two have always been solid."

A giant lump forms in my throat. I can't even bring myself to try to swallow it down. There's so much she doesn't know. Even more I don't understand yet. "Marriage is complicated, sweetheart."

"Yeah, well, so is calculus, but Dad doesn't sleep on the couch over that."

"Dad never passed algebra." Despite myself, I laugh and reach out to playfully punch her arm. "You're too smart for your own good."

She smiles faintly. "Whatever it is..." She trails off, choosing her words slowly. "He looks sad, and not like his regular sad when his terrible Voltage team loses. This is deeper."

"This is not something I need to talk to you about." I tug one side of my lips into a smile, forcing some positivity in my tone. "I appreciate your concern, but it'll work out as it's supposed to."

Her eyes pace around my face as concern grows in the lines on her forehead. "Are you sure there isn't something I can do to help?"

Her empathy is making my knot balloon even more. I pat her leg and smile bigger, though it tugs at my heart to be so deceitful. "Yeah, it's a minor thing." Tears spring in my eyes, and out of panic, I quickly point to the alarm clock glowing next to my bed. "It's late. We should get some sleep."

"Right." Disappointment etches her whole face, but it doesn't stop her from leaning forward, hugging me. "Night."

"Night, sweetie." She pulls away and shuffles across the room, quietly closing the door behind her. My attention turns out the darkened window across from my bed, and on my faint reflection peering back at me.

It wasn't right to lie to her.

I've never been one of those moms who thinks it's better to protect kids from the truth. In time, she will find out more, but she doesn't need to know everything, because in truth, I don't know what's really going on.

I know I'm sad.

A new emotion for me. As before when I moved out, I was mad and fed up. I'm over the frustration of the situation. My professional opinion would say it's the normal progression of the stages of grief, and I'm almost to the next, the final one—acceptance.

That I'm clearly not at yet.

It wasn't hard for me to decide to take a break from the marriage. My anger had been boiling over for years, but if I take any more steps forward with separation, it's going to affect my entire family.

Every Christmas from here on out.

Every birthday.

Even the kids' weddings.

What about grandkids?

I hate to be that person who splits her family.

I don't even believe in divorce. I'm not sure I'd even go so far as to make anything legal. I don't want that. I just want to stop feeling so broken. My heart is so divided, it's like it's a country at war with itself. Neither side is making any headway.

I don't know which path is worse.

One way, I lose my old life completely, or on the off chance, I let myself hope again...it might just break me for good, especially now that Blake has *another* project he's working on with this team. I don't know what he's thinking about adding one more GIANT thing to come between us. I thought a break would make him see how much he lost, but he just filled that hole with something else, like I didn't even exist. Even strong marriages suffer when a new business is being built. There's no way our shattered relationship can weather any more stress. The worst part is, he never even asked me what I thought about it. He was just headstrong, making decisions, spending our money, like we are already permanently separated. It's that exact behavior, him just living his life full-steam ahead without me, that got us here. He's digging himself an even bigger hole and doesn't have the slightest idea how it pains me to see him put so much energy into that, and nothing into us.

Sure, he put on a good show for Noah and Paisley.

I don't think he's capable of changing for good.

Twenty-Six

BLAKE

Inside my gym office, a shadow passes in front of the door, and I hear, "Hey, Dad. Would you want to run down to the lake cabin with me this weekend?"

I glance up from my laptop. I've been lucky enough to see Peyton nearly every day since he started working in the mornings, but he hasn't asked to do anything together outside of the gym, in well, years. Usually, he's too busy with friends and whichever girlfriend he has at the time. "Sure," I say, then soften my tone, "Is everything okay?"

He shrugs, but it does nothing to give any emotion away. "I thought it would be good to get away for a while, and I miss hanging out there. You know what I mean?"

That's all it takes. If one of my boys needs me, I'm there. No hesitation.

"Yeah, that sounds nice. Let's do it." I give a bigger than needed nod and wait for him to offer more information.

"Sweet, I'll bring my ice fishing gear. There's bound to be something biting."

"Yeah, I could go fishing." I cross my arms and lean back in my chair, giving him my full attention. As much as it's nice to get away, this is so unlike him. He lives with his two brothers, and they are the ones who do everything together, not usually asking their old man to hang out. Unless they aren't getting along? Maybe that's it? Since Peyton got kicked off the team, those other two might be leaving him out.

"Did you want to ask Mom if she can come too?"

There it is.

Is he picking up on the tension and hinting at something? "I can," I start slowly, wondering how I'm going to talk my way out of this. "But you know she's not going to sit outside in the cold. Actually, it's sort of perfect, because Paisley is back at home, and those two will more than likely want to do some girl activity." I wave my hand in a dismissive manner. "They won't even notice I'm gone."

"If you think so." Looking over his shoulder, he backs out of my doorway, calling out, "I have a client standing in the doorway, but we'll plan more later."

"Sounds good." As he strides away, my mind returns to his question about asking Lacey. My gaze immediately drops to the floor. She won't come. Sure, she'd love to hang out with Peyton, but if I'm there, she'll definitely choose to stay at the house with Paisley. I blow out a breath and sigh. Life isn't how I dreamed it would be, but I'm grateful Peyton hasn't given up on me. It is sus though that he's bringing all this up now. Maybe he feels sorry for me?

Twenty-Seven

LACEY

Rushing to get out the door for work, I fly down the stairs to find Paisley in the kitchen with a piece of toast in one hand and her phone in the other. "Oh hey, honey," I greet her as I pivot around her to get to the coffeepot to fill up my to-go mug. "What do you have going on today?"

"Job hunting, actually. You know, since I quit working for Dad, I need to find something to do. I have some photography clients, but it's slower than I thought it should be." She leans against the counter and sets her phone screen down in front of her. "I'm glad I caught you before you left for work. I was thinking, we could do a little mother-daughter weekend. Just us. It's been forever, and I could use some time with you. I know you could help me figure out what to do next."

Her eyes shimmer with earnestness that tugs at my heart, and I don't even stop to think. "Of course. Anywhere you want to go?" I put my lip on my cup and turn toward her to give her my full attention.

"Well, I thought about that too, but I don't have any money, remember? So, I thought maybe a lazy weekend at the lake cabin. We haven't been there in forever, and it's just sitting empty. We can pack a bunch of junk food, maybe some movies and just relax."

Warmth lifts through me. I love our little family lake cabin. It's not much, but it's been in my family for decades. Though we use it less and less each year, it was a solid weekend hangout for the whole family when the kids were younger. It's a great spot to reconnect with her and help her through this next stage of her career. Plus, if I'm honest, I love the idea of not having to tiptoe around Blake at the house. It's the perfect weekend plan. Blake's so busy with this new team, he won't even notice we're gone. "That's phenomenal. I can have everything packed the night before, get off work by four, and we can hit the road."

"Perfect." Her smile fills her whole face. "I'll be waiting and ready."

Crossing the room, I grab my winter coat from the rack, slipping it on as I open the door, "I'll talk to you tonight, honey. Have a great day." I slip out as her bye echoes, and my heart soars. It's been a long time since I've had weekend plans. I love having Paisley home again. As much as I was happy for her to have her own place, and pursue her own life, family has always meant everything to me. This will be the best weekend.

Twenty-Eight

BLAKE

The loose gravel crunches under my pickup tires as I turn around the final bend in the road. My headlights catch the wooden sign that's been hanging crooked since Lacey first brought me out to meet her parents here, all those years ago. Rocky Ridge Cabin. Nostalgia swishes in my stomach. It's been years since I've been this far upstate, but the scent of pine pitch hits my memory just right.

"Dad," Peyton says from the passenger seat. "Are you ready to catch some fish tomorrow?"

"Uh-huh." I ease the truck into the driveway crowded with low-hanging evergreen branches that need to be trimmed. "Absolutely. I hope the bass are biting."

His face is illuminated by the lights on the dash, and I catch his grin growing. "Yeah, no oversleeping. Be ready to leave for the dock at five at the latest. If you're not ready, I'll head out without you."

I turn into the approach, and my lights flash on a familiar license plate already in the driveway. I freeze. There's no doubt about it. Lacey's car. It has a recognizable dent on the passenger side door from when she backed into a pole a couple of years ago. "Peyton," I say slowly, "why is your mother's car here on our guys' weekend?"

"Uh... maybe she—uh—got lost?" He looks out the door, scanning around, obviously doing everything he can to avoid looking at me.

"We both know she didn't get lost in upstate New York." I glare at him for a second. "Did you tell her we were coming?"

Before he can reply, the cabin door flies open, and the humble porch light casts a golden halo around Lacey. She's wearing a soft gray sweater, matching sweatpants, and those ugly brown boots she had on her Christmas list. Refusing to buy them for her, I told her they were too country looking. She was lucky Paisley said they look like they were made for a Hallmark movie, and she gifted them to her.

She might have been more right than me. Both of them.

My breath catches before I can stop it.

Lacey looks stunning as a country girl.

I slide off my seat, shut the door, and cautiously fix my gaze on Lacey. Her expression flickers between confusion and horror as her eyes widen comically huge.

"What are you doing here?" we blurt at the exact same time.

I swear she's going to laugh. Instead, she presses a hand to her forehead and stares past me. "Peyton, you have got to be kidding me!"

Behind me, Peyton clears his throat, throwing his hand up like he's ready to celebrate. "Uh, surprise?"

And there it is. The realization crashes in. Clearly, we aren't as smooth as we thought we were about hiding this separation. The kids not only caught on, but they conspired against us. "Oh, those sneaky little traitors," I mutter, not really caring who hears me. I'm not stupid. I keep my face neutral as I pretend to be annoyed. I don't want Lacey to think I had anything to do with this, but inside my heart is slamming against my chest. Why didn't I think to involve the kids sooner? Had I known they would help get us back together—as they should—I'd have confided in Peyton months ago.

From inside the cabin, a second voice pipes up, and I'm smiling when I hear. "Mom? Who are you talking to?" And then Paisley steps out, carrying an oversized mug of something piping hot. She freezes mid-step when she sees me, and goes into actress mode, very badly pretending to be shocked. "Oh! Wow! Dad! What a coincidence."

She's a terrible liar.

Peyton jumps in, speaking in a too-loud voice, "Yeah, total coincidence. We just thought, you know, it'd be cool if Dad and I got away for the weekend."

Lacey crosses her arms, her gaze cutting from Peyton back to Paisley. "You two planned this?"

They exchange some silent sibling telepathy look between them. Paisley bites her lip as she slowly speaks, "Define *planned*?"

"Define busted for lying," Lacey fires back.

I can't help it, but I laugh. My chest inflates with hope that I haven't felt in a long time. It's short-lived though, as Lacey shoots me a look that could peel paint. "Oh, don't you dare laugh. This is your fault too, somehow. I can feel it."

I raise my hands. "Hey, all I know is Peyton asked to go fishing. I brought groceries and fishing poles. I had no idea this was up his sleeve..." I stop myself before I blurt out how happy I am to see her. With the way her arms cross over her chest, and she's glaring at Peyton, it's quite clear she is not happy to see me.

"Well, it's too late for anyone to head back to Long Island tonight." Peyton shifts on his feet before he goes around to the back of my truck, lowers the tailgate, and then says, "So, we should probably settle in for the night."

Lacey exhales, muttering something under her breath as she turns to go inside. I grab the cooler from the back seat, mostly because I need something to do besides stare after her. Peyton grabs both of our bags, and we amble up the broken pathway together. Despite the setup, I'm glad to be back here.

The cabin looks exactly how I remember it, with honey-colored knotty pine walls and the big stone fireplace blackened from years of use. A buck head still hangs crooked above the mantel. It was one of her dad's trophies from when she was little. I could easily reach up and straighten it, but it's something about the character it brings to the place to have it off-kilter. It's always been like that since I've started coming here. It's definitely cozy. With only one bedroom and an oversized sleeping loft we used to let the kids pile in with sleeping bags, I hate to even ask about the sleeping arrangements.

Or maybe hate is the wrong word?

I glance at the closed door to the only bedroom, where Lacey and I spent so many nights, a slow grin tugging at my mouth. I'm not sure what the right word is to describe my current emotional status, but it's not hate. Suddenly, heat blooms through my chest. I'm all sparkly nerved as I think about this one-bed situation waiting to happen.

Lacey taps her foot, hands on hips, while I set the cooler on the only kitchen counter. "Well, this should be interesting." The sarcasm practically drips.

Paisley blurts out, "It was too short of notice to get Paul and Preston to come, but we thought it was a nice surprise to have some family time."

"Don't pretend like we don't all know what's going on. Let's be adults here." Lacey sighs while pinching the bridge of her nose. "You two are lucky I love you so much."

There's a long, awkward silence, the kind that feels like standing at the edge of a cliff, before Peyton claps his hands together. "Great! So, I'll let Paisley have the loft. I can grab the sofa, and you two can have your room."

Lacey mutters, "Oh, for crying out loud," and stalks toward the exit, not stopping until she's out on the porch again.

I follow her, mostly out of habit, and lean against the doorway as she starts pacing back and forth on the creaking wood boards. She glances over her shoulder. "If I find out you had anything to do with this," she hisses, "I'll be letting the air out of all four of your tires, so you are stranded here forever."

I grin. Nothing can ruin my good mood. "I get cell phone reception out here now."

She shoots me with a conspiratorial side-eye. "I'll throw that phone in the lake."

Behind me, I faintly hear the kids rummaging through my cooler. "You realize they're not sorry."

She heaves out a sigh. "Not even a little."

We stand here for a beat as the silence fills in with the soft creak of crickets. "Did you tell them?" she finally asks.

"Nope. Not a word."

"Well, one of them figured something out." She glances up at me, and her eyes soften. "We might as well confess everything to clear the air. Tell them we are separated, and this plan isn't going to sway us."

A sucker punch lands in my gut. I don't know why that thought hadn't occurred to me. I guess I got caught up in the nostalgia of being back here. My mind had us all making s'mores around the fire. What a fool I was for thinking this would change anything. My chest cinches so tightly, I can barely breathe out, "Please, Lacey. Not tonight. They went through all of this trouble to get us here. If our family is going to change forever, can we make one more memory for their sake?"

She halts her pacing, her gaze impatiently bouncing around my face. I hold my breath as one more memory doesn't seem fair. I had promised a lifetime of them, but I guess I wasn't enough for her.

"Sure," she quips. "It's late anyway. We can avoid the issue like we've been doing for one more day. But it's time. I've put this off for too long. We'll make our official announcement in the morning before Paisley and I head back to town."

"Tomorrow?" A swallow pulses through my throat, as a nervous tick twitches through my hand, causing me to scrub over the back of my neck. "I figured you were staying the weekend."

"We were going to, but really, come on, Blake." Her head tips to the side. "Did you really think we can all hang out here in this tiny cabin?"

Feeling foolish now, I drop my gaze.

Because I did for some reason hope that would happen.

Maybe I'm as naïve as the kids are, but I've never been one to give up until the final buzzer sounds. Until my last breath, I'm holding on to hope that we'll recover. We have too much history not to. Knowing better than to pull some big romantic speech, I stay quiet. She turns her back and gazes out over the porch, making it clear she's done listening to me.

She may think she ended this conversation, but I'm not wasting the opportunity. If this is the last time we spend together as a family, I'm giving it my everything. I'm going to do something more subtly romantic like a fire. The kind of fire a man builds for the woman he loves, and that makes her crave snuggling for hours. While she's still stewing on the porch, I stride into the living room, roll up my sleeves, and declare, "It's time for the fire!"

Paisley, who is curled on the couch, raises an eyebrow. She doesn't even try to hide her smirk. "Fire?"

"Yeah," I say with confidence that's about to bite me. "I'll build us a fire for a cozy night in."

Her lips quirk even more. "Did you ask Mom first?"

"I don't have to ask your mom's permission to build a fire in our family cabin," I mutter as I pull a log out of the basket.

I have no idea how long the logs have even been sitting in there, because I've never chopped wood in my life. The fire was always something Lacey did, but it's time I step up. I drop the log into the fireplace and grab kindling. I've seen this done thousands of times. It can't be hard. I strike a match and hold it up to a twig, and like I planned, the twig glows with a flame. I blow out the match and slowly move the twig closer to the log, waiting for the flame to transfer.

And it's perfect.

It takes a couple of minutes for the flame to take hold, but the log slowly burns, bringing warmth into the room. Leaning back on my heels, I marvel at it. When I'm pleased, I call out, "Somebody grab the stuff for s'mores. We are in business!"

Then it happens.

Instead of whisking upward, the smoke barrels straight into the room.

Lacey comes in from outside with wide eyes and instantly starts coughing. "Did you open the chimney?"

"What?" I try to conceal my wave over the smoke, coughing myself. "Why would it be closed?" I rasp. My eyes start to sting, as I grope for the lever, yanking on the flue like it's a slot machine. It creaks like it's mad at me. After a good tug, the smoke starts pulling up instead of out. Lacey sighs as she stomps her feet to the window and heaves it open. She's coughing and swatting at the haze as she tries to clear the air.

I fall back on my heels, soot smudged on my shirt. My pride is toast.

"Smooth one, Dad." Paisley says, wiping at the corner of her eyes with the bottom of her sweatshirt. "Very smooth."

"Just trying to keep it interesting," I wheeze as I pound on the front of my chest with my fist.

"Interesting?" Peyton chimes in, his tone is laced with snickers. "You almost set the place on fire."

Lacey grabs a heavy throw blanket from the couch and wraps it over her shoulders as she pivots on her heel, calling over her shoulder, "I'm heading back to the porch until the smoke clears. Who's coming out with me?"

"I'll join you," Paisley coughs out as she follows her. Peyton is right on their heels too. They file out the door, leaving me to sit alone in front of this smoking log as I try to clean this cabin up from the mess I made. Somewhere in this mess there's a metaphor to describe how this fits perfectly into what I did with my life, but I can't find the words to make sense. Instead, I use my hands to steer the smoke up the chimney and watch as my family gathers on the porch without me.

I'm not a crier, but a single hot tear forms, pressing on the back of my eyelid. It's actually surprising I haven't broken down and bawled even once through these past months, but I've stayed so busy, scheming up plans to win Lacey back, to really allow the feeling of loss to sink in. It's unavoidable now. My family turns their backs on me.

It feels like my family's future just went up in smoke.

I wouldn't wish this feeling of deep heartbreak on Bill Baker.

Every dream I had for us just... stopped breathing

Twenty-Nine

Lacey

A fog of smoke seeps from the cracked window, curling into the night air. The porch light catches the haze, turning it silver against the dark pines. I'm bundled in a red flannel blanket on the old porch swing, trying not to laugh every time Blake mutters, "It wasn't that bad. I had it under control."

"It was that bad," I say, biting back a grin. "You filled the entire cabin with smoke." I'm laughing outside. Inside I'm stewing. I can't help but think *this is so like Blake*. Thinking he has control and his problems aren't anything too bad. If he says it's not an issue, then it's not an issue, and he never considers how other people feel. He completely forgets there are two people in our marriage, one of which needs his love, and you can't just brush that desire away like chimney smoke. He thinks everything is a quick fix, and he doesn't stop to ask what his role is in anything.

He spreads his hands in front of him. "In my defense, the wood was damp."

"The wood was old," Paisley chimes in as she pulls the hood up on her hoodie, tugging the strings tight. "Dad, it's time to admit it. You didn't know what you were doing. It's not a big deal." Paisley tucks her knees up like she's still struggling to get warm in the rickety wooden rocking chair. It's a tad colder out here than what's comfortable, and everyone is shivering. "This reminds me of that camping trip when you tried to roast hot dogs on wooden sticks."

Throwing back his head of overgrown hair, Peyton groans, "Don't get me started on that Yellowstone trip. He set the entire picnic table on fire."

I blink and peer at Peyton. "What picnic table?"

"Uh oh." Peyton glances at his sister, and they grin. "We weren't supposed to tell Mom about that, were we?"

Blake's eyes widen as his hand flies out in a defensive gesture. "It was a small fire. Barely even—"

"Small?" Paisley laughs as her hands start to flow with her words in animated gestures. "You melted the new cooler!"

"How am I only hearing about this now?" I stare at them as my jaw falls. "Where was I?"

"It was when you took a walk." Blake's grin is sheepish. "I didn't want to worry you."

"Uh-huh." Crossing my arms tighter, I avoid his eye contact and look up at the sky, finding a few bright stars peeking out from the otherwise dark night. "What else didn't you tell me?"

"Don't ask if you don't want to know," Peyton whispers as a playful tone etches in.

"What? There's more?" I can't help but drop my gaze, hooking his direct eye contact. Peyton and I have always been close. I thought he told me everything. "I want to hear what else there is."

Peyton grins ear to ear as he coaxes, "You sure about that, Mom?"

"Positive. You might as well confess. You can't get in trouble anymore now that you're grown."

It's quiet for the longest time before Paisley cracks. "Fine. I'll start. Remember junior year when I said I stayed at Brooke's house after the homecoming football game?"

Blakes eyes immediately darken as they laser on her. "Please tell me this story doesn't end with a boy."

She bursts out laughing. "No boy, but I wasn't at Brooke's. And I didn't go to homecoming. I was in New York City for a concert."

"You mean the concert we *forbade* you to go to?" I try not to laugh. I can't help it. Paisley was always a rule follower. I would expect this confession from any of her brothers but not her.

Blake's hand flies to his forehead as if he's struck a fever. "Oh, for crying out loud, Paisley. You were what, sixteen? What were you thinking?" Before she replies, Blake looks at me, acting all serious. "Are you sure it's not too late to ground her?"

I chuckle. There isn't anything else to do about it. That was years ago. I'm not happy to learn about it. In a way, it's not as stressful hearing about it now, as she clearly lived through it. Evidenced by the fact she is sitting in front of me.

Peyton gives me that mischievous grin. "All right, Mom. Your turn."

I feign offense. "Me?"

He slants his index finger toward me, incriminating me for something I have no idea of. "You."

I tap my chin dramatically. "I don't do anything that isn't perfect—"

"No, that's not true!" Peyton speaks over me. "Why don't you tell Dad the real reason the mailbox disappeared."

Blake squints at me, his expression growing hard. "The mailbox that was stolen?"

"Yeah," I say, grinning as my cheeks heat. Boy, had I known this was what my weekend was going to consist of, I'd have slashed my own tires so we couldn't make it up here. Shaking my head, I ponder an excuse, but at this point, there's no reason to lie. "I might have run it over."

Paisley gasps. "Isn't that illegal?"

"Are you serious?" Blake blurts out. "I worried for weeks that someone got our mail." He looks at me with mock disbelief. "So, let me get this straight. You've been lying for ten years?"

I shrug. "It wasn't really a lie. I took care of it and got a new one." I'm chuckling while Blake deadpans on me.

"That's unreal," Blake mutters.

"Okay, I've got one." Peyton's tone softens, cueing us all in to be quiet. "But it's not funny. When I dropped out of college last year," he says slowly, "it wasn't just because I failed my classes. I was really struggling. I didn't want to tell you guys, because I didn't want to disappoint you."

My chest tightens. I immediately recall a few late-night calls I brushed off as him just being bored, because they were always followed by the quick texts that said *I'm fine.* "What do you mean?" I whisper.

He shrugs. "I'm fine now. I was dating this girl. It sounds silly, but she broke up with me. It really messed me up. Then school was piling on, and the coach hated me. I just needed a fresh start. Just, looking back, I should've said something."

No one speaks for a beat. Then Blake leans forward, placing a hand on his shoulder. "You're right. You should have said something. I'm sorry you went through that alone."

Paisley reaches over from the other side and playfully nudges her brother's arm. "You know I'm here for you too."

"Thanks." The tension breaks enough for him to add a grin that does nothing to convince my mama heart he's okay, and he stands and stretches. "Okay, that's enough emotional damage for one night. It looks like the cabin is mostly aired out. I'm exhausted since I got up at four to open the gym. If it's all right, I'm heading to bed."

Paisley's phone rings, the screen lighting up her face. "It's Noah," she says, hopping up too. "I'll take this call inside."

And just like that, they disappear through the creaky screen door, and the porch feels wider without their voices. I sit here, staring into the dark sky, a lump in my throat swelling as I ponder what Peyton really meant. He said he was okay now. I don't believe him. He wouldn't bring it up if he was over it. I've talked to a lot of kids in my career. Sometimes that's just a last cry for help.

Blake exhales beside me. "He should've told us."

"I should've noticed," I whisper. "He was telling us in a hundred little ways, but I was brushing them off. I'm trained to see all the signs. Now looking back, they were there. He'd call me so many times at the most random hours. I bought his excuse that he was bored."

"You had no idea of really knowing."

"I'm his mom. I should have known." I look at him. Tears prick the back of my eyes before I can stop them. "I blamed you for not being around enough and missing things, but here I was missing things too. Huge things."

The last of the smoke drifts out the cabin window like a ghost of everything we've burned and survived. I can't help but think if maybe part of the reason Peyton planned to get together this weekend was so maybe we'd slow down and really see him. After a long silence, Blake says the very thing I'm thinking, "We can't change what we missed, but it's not too late to try now."

My breath shudders out. "Yeah, he said he was fine, but that's usually a cry for help. Something is still going on. We just have to get him to trust us."

Blake's eyes fill with sincerity. "And how do we do that?"

"By being here for him." I nod with conviction. "We don't leave until he opens up." I stare at Blake, hoping he agrees. I don't have a good feeling about this. I'm not leaving Peyton alone until I know he's okay. This is the part where I put my foot down, and Blake usually grumbles about having to get back to work the next day or needing to watch the hockey game. To my surprise, his eyes lock on mine.

All he says is, "You're right." Goosebumps spiral up my spine as the lump in my throat continues to swell. I fight the urge to march back into that cabin and force Peyton to talk.

That won't earn his trust. He's always been more of a gentle soul. He'll come to me when he's ready. It might take time, but I'm prepared to camp out here as long as he needs.

Even if it means I'm stuck with Blake.

Thirty

BLAKE

The cabin door clicks shut behind us, muting the wind to a low purr against the withering side. I stand still, inhaling the scent of woodsmoke. Sure, it's a little more potent than I'd care for it to be, but it brings a wave of nostalgia gushing through. It's the smell of every winter school break we've ever spent here, every Christmas, and even summer vacations with the kids.

Out of the corner of my eye, I spot Paisley up in the loft, curled up on the pullout. She's half-buried under a blanket that barely shows her dark hair peeking out. For a second, it's easy to pretend she's still a child. It's funny how when we were in the thick of it, I thought our lives would never slow down. This is the first time in months—really since Paisley graduated high school—I've spent any time with her.

Down below the loft, Peyton's sprawled on the only couch with his bare arm dangling off the side. His phone is directly below his hand like he got too tired scrolling and fell asleep mid-video.

I nod toward them and whisper, "It feels good to have them sleeping under the same roof again. I didn't realize I missed it. Too bad Paul and Preston couldn't have made it."

"Yeah." Lacey's chuckle is quiet. "Guess all that family time wore them out."

Family time.

The words land heavier than she probably meant them to. We used to always make time to do things together, but as each kid moved out, family time became a less regular thing. They had their lives, and I took advantage of the extra time to work more. Looking back, I was basically completely ignoring Lacey. I assumed we were good. I mean, I knew I was good and still as in love as I always was.

Maybe just blind too?

Also, I was really stupid to take her for granted. I hate it took her moving out to open my eyes. My gaze drifts past her to the closed bedroom door.

It's *our* bedroom.

At least it used to be, and it's the only available bed left. I scratch at the back of my neck and whisper, "Well, I can sleep in the truck." I nod toward the window, where frost now crawls up the glass from the fast-dipping temps. "It's only, what, thirty degrees?"

"That seems a little dramatic." She turns to me with one of her brows raised. "Don't you think?"

"I'll survive."

She smiles, faintly, then sighs. "It's not a big deal. We can share our bed for one night. The kids might worry about you out there in the cold. Peyton seems to have enough going on. He doesn't need to stress about you freezing to death."

She's right. I have no idea what's going on with that kid. The last thing he needs is to wake up and see his dad's kicked out in the snow. So I nod, because arguing feels wrong. "If you insist."

Inching toward our room, we cross the threshold together. She clicks a lamp at her bedside table. It's modern but meant to look like an antique kerosene lamp. The kids always loved playing with it when they were little, pretending they were out camping in the wilderness. Something in me twists at how little this room has changed. Her dresser mirror is still cluttered with photos pinned all around the frame. It's all memories of summer floating down the lake and waking up late mornings with bedhead smiles. Lacey steps right up to the mirror and brushes her fingers over the corner of one photo. I pause as her reflection shines back. It's impossible to miss her eyes, glassy under the lamplight. "Hard to believe that was all of us," she says quietly. "The kids were so small. Now they are all grown and gone."

I want to say I miss it. I would go back in a heartbeat, but she doesn't need to hear me whine. Instead, I pull my shirt over my head and grab a blanket and pillow from the closet. "I'll just be down here," I say, dropping my bedding to the wood floor.

"Don't be ridiculous." She blinks, appearing confused. "Your back will never recover."

"I've slept in worse places than this," I mutter under my breath, a little too quiet for her to hear.

She folds her arms, watching me spread the blanket. "Blake, it's just a bed. It's fine. I've birthed four of your kids. You're not going to scandalize me. I think we can be mature adults for one night."

I glance up at her, trying for a smirk. "You sure? I snore, apparently."

"Yeah." There's the tiniest tug of a smile. "I remember."

She grabs her flannel pajama pants and a fuzzy sweatshirt from her bag and turns her back to me to change. I retrieve my pillow and blanket and spread them on the left side of the bed, and stare at it like I'm seeing this bed for the first time.

It's big enough for two.

I give in and slide onto the far side, lying stiff as a soldier. When she turns around, her steps falter as her eyes unmissably widen like she wasn't expecting me to listen to her suggestion of sharing the bed. Then she exhales, walks over, climbs in, and lies down while keeping her back toward me.

My breath hitches in my throat as the mattress dips slightly under her weight. I catch the faintest scent of her shampoo. It's something sweet I could never name but always knew. When I inhale, I close my eyes, hold her scent, so afraid this may be the very last time I can do this. It's so unbelievably heartbreaking how I used to take moments like these for granted. Now it feels like the highest privilege.

I exhale, allowing myself to absorb her nearness.

"Thank you," she whispers.

"For what?" My voice comes out raspy.

"For agreeing with me about staying for Peyton."

I open my eyes to the ceiling. I'm careful not to encroach on her space, and I avoid looking at her directly and watch the shadows shifting in the moonlight that shines through the only window. I say the most honest thing I've said all year, "There's nowhere else I'd rather be."

She doesn't answer, but I don't miss the slight shaking of her shoulders. Then she goes still again, breathing slowly. I don't even try to sleep. I can't give away this moment. I stare at the soft rise and fall of her back and think that maybe, for one night, this old cabin's doing what it always did best. It brings us together when we've forgotten how.

Please, let it work this time.

Thirty-One

LACEY

Solid warmth presses along my back, and the heaviness of an arm around my waist pulls me from my sleep. For a moment, I forget where I am as I'm so cozy and warm.

And then it hits me.

I'm in the cabin.

In the same bed as Blake.

The arm around me belongs to *him*!

My eyes pop open, and I blink as the sheer curtains leaking in the early morning light, and dust floats lazily in the air.

The old clock on the nightstand glows that it's not even seven yet. When I dare to look at Blake's hand, I hold my breath. It's splayed against my stomach. Somewhere in the night we found each other exactly the way we always used to. Oddly, it doesn't make me cringe the way I would have thought. I stay still, hoping he doesn't wake just yet and retreat inside my head. This cabin just pulls the memories out of me.

Summer mornings when the kids were little, when he'd wake me up by brushing his cold nose against my shoulder. I'd pretend to be annoyed. The way we'd all pile into this very bed on Christmas morning. We'd all be tangled in blankets and laughter with the kids begging to open presents right now.

It all feels like another lifetime.

I blink up at the photos still pinned around my mirror, their edges curled from years of sunlight. All the sunburns and smiles this cabin has seen will never be enough for me.

I would do it all again.

And again after that.

I could relive my kids' childhoods over and over for a hundred lifetimes, and it would still be gone too fast.

Blake's breath loudly blows out, pulling my gaze back to his face. It's not quite a full snore, but it's loud enough to make me shake my head. Oddly, I'm not annoyed. My chest tightens into some kind of discomfort I don't recognize. He shifts, and his eyes open. A confused sound catches in his throat, and he sits halfway up before he jerks his hand back like he's been burned. "Oh—sorry," he mutters, his voice rough from sleep. "I didn't—"

"It's fine." I roll over, forcing a small smile even though my heart's still pounding. His eyes meet mine for the briefest second before he swings his legs off the bed and swiftly gets up, grabs the first shirt he can find, and pulls it over his head. I sit up, tucking my knees under the quilt. "You don't have to be embarrassed," I say softly.

He rakes a hand through his hair, avoiding my gaze like the floorboards have suddenly become fascinating. I toy with the idea of saying something nice to him, because as confusing as this moment is, it feels safe.

The door bursts open. Paisley flies in with her dark hair sticking up in every direction. "Mom! Dad!" she blurts, wide-eyed. "Peyton's gone."

"What?" I yawn, a little sleepy.

"He's not on the couch," she says breathlessly. "His shoes are gone, and his phone's not there. There's snow tracks all the way out toward the woods."

I'm already out of bed, tripping over the blanket as I kick out of it. A tidal wave of panic crashes into my heart, revving it up and stilling it all at once. That doesn't sound like Peyton. He's not one to go off by himself, especially in the cold. Blake's jaw tightens as we stare at each other. Panic continues to seep from my heart, all through my body, burning hotter than anything I've ever felt.

"I'll find him." Blake charges forward and yells back, "You guys stay here in case he comes back. Don't leave."

I'm frozen in place, but my mother instinct kicks in. I want to run after Peyton too, but I fight against that urge. Forcing myself to stay calm for Paisley, I let out a shaky breath as I pace to the living room and examine the place for clues.

Paisley's right.

There's nothing but tracks from our front door headed out to the forest. Before I can process any more, Blake's thrown his coat and boots on, and he flings open the front door, calling back, "I'll bring him home."

Thirty-Two

Blake

Frigid air hits me the second I step outside. I've never been more thankful for snow. The fresh layer caught every tread of prints leading away from the cabin into the trees. "Come on, bud," I mutter under my breath as I tug my jacket closed. My breath puffs out in a pale cloud, and whispers, "What is going on with you?"

Every step crunches loudly, and I trudge down the trail where the pines huddle close together and the ground dips toward the lake. I take comfort in the fact his tracks are steady.

There's no sign of running or panic, and they veer toward the frozen water.

A soft *hoot* breaks the silence. I jump before realizing it's just an owl perched low on a branch, staring at me like I'm an idiot. "Yeah, yeah," I mutter, placing a hand over my chest. "You got me."

My heart's pounding as I break through the tree line, and the lake opens up before me. The sun's cresting enough to turn everything silver. I survey the area and almost cry out in relief as the constriction in my heart finally gives. About twenty feet out on the ice, Peyton's hunched over a small ice fishing hole. He's smartly bundled in his parka and knit hat. A little tackle box sits open next to him. I pant as I continue to stride forward and call out, "Peyton!"

He turns, tossing his hand up in a wave, and replies, "Morning."

My boots crunch across the snow-crusted edge of the lake, and I halt before the ice. "Are you trying to give your mother a heart attack by taking off and not telling anyone?"

"What are you talking about heart attack? I told you last night I was going fishing in the morning." He shrugs, staring down at the hole. "I said if you're late again, I'd leave without you."

"Right..." My voice trails off as I remember now. He's not lying. We had made plans to fish. That was before I knew the girls were joining us, and before I accidentally snuggled with

Lacey and lost my ability to think straight. "I, ah, so sorry. I forgot we made plans. I got all mixed up. I didn't mean to ditch you."

"I'm used to it." His voice is so low.

Ouch. That stings, but it might be the most honest thing he's ever said. I've been guilty of pushing off plans with Lacey and the kids for another client or a hockey game that ran into overtime. It's like a veil has finally lifted, and I see so clearly how wrong that was. I feel terrible for missing our planned father/son time. I crouch near the shore, resting my elbows on my knees, and study him. "Sorry. You want to tell me what's going on?"

His eyes remain fixed on the hole, but I don't miss the twitching in his jaw. That's the real giveaway I need to know he's close to talking. "Just needed to think."

"I understand that." I try my hardest to keep my voice even, but I'm uncomfortable in this role. I've never been the one to initiate these hard conversations with the kids. Since Lacey is the professional counselor, I gladly punted every tough talk to her. From friends, to dating, to poor grades and even money management, she was the best at all of it. Tilting my head to the side, I let my guilt sink. That's just another way I wasn't there for her and the kids. How lonely Lacey had to be. I'm just so bad at this talking stuff. I'm more of a worker, but I get that doesn't let me off the hook anymore. I need to try something to save my boy. Blowing out a breath, I think back to all the things I've heard Lacey say, and I pull out her favorite line, she says on repeat. "You know, your mom always says when you are overwhelmed and have trouble thinking that it's maybe time to ask for help."

"I know she says that all the time. It's so annoying." He rolls his eyes and lingers in a long beat of silence before he says, barely above a whisper, "I messed up, Dad."

"What do you mean?" I blurt out as my stomach tightens. I honestly hadn't planned on this approach working. He never opens up to me, but now my heart motors into overdrive as my mind flashes all the ways a college kid can get in trouble. Just as I open my mouth to spout off, he winces and turns his head away from me, and I get it.

He doesn't need a lecture or a tough parent. He needs a friend, and I close my mouth, swallow, and start again. This time more calmly, "It's okay, son. Everyone messes up sometimes. What kind of messed up are we talking about?"

He raises his shoulders, holding his gaze on the hole. "You're going to be mad." His voice cracks, and he clears it. "I was upset about this girl, the one I told you about. I was out with some friends, and I saw her with another guy. I left because I got so upset. I didn't want to accidentally run into her. When I got to my car, her car was parked right next to mine. It felt like she did it on purpose. You know, like she wanted me to see it. I got furious and kicked her taillights until they busted, but I guess the parking lot had cameras."

My breath leaves me in a fog. All my boys are tough and played hockey for years, but of the three of them, Peyton was always the most level-headed. I honestly can't see him doing that. Tipping my head to the side, I sit in the memory, and I can clearly see *me* doing that in my hot-headed twenties.

But not him.

He's undoubtedly hurt and acting out of character. Before I reply, he rushes out, "I know. I know it was stupid. I have a court date this week..." His voice trails off as he hangs his head so low, I can only see the start of his hairline.

I've never been an overly affectionate dad. At least not with my boys. I wanted them to be tough. Something catches in my chest, like putting on display yet another one of my failures. I don't want to continue to fail everyone, and I cautiously step across the ice until I reach him. My hand lands on his shoulder. "Hey, look at me."

He raises his gaze to mine, guilt swirling in his eyes. It sits there heavy, like he's waiting for me to scold him. Every instinct in me screams to pull him into my arms and promise him everything will be fine.

But I can't really make those promises.

As a parent you want to protect your child, but choices have consequences. He'll likely have restitution and charges applied to his record. It stinks starting your adult life off like that. I know a few judges, and I could make some calls...

My fingers curl against my palms, nails biting into skin as I fight the urge to fix it for him. I've always been good at that part—patching cracks, pretending the fractures aren't deep enough to matter, avoiding the punishment, finding someone else to blame.

That again, is part of my problem. It needs to stop. I need to be accountable, and I need to let my boys be accountable too, so they don't repeat my same pattern. "I'm a little shocked but not going to lecture you. You're an adult," I say quietly as my fingers continue to squeeze into fists as I hold back my urge to raise my voice. "But I also won't pretend it didn't happen either."

His shoulders sag, like the weight he's been carrying finally found somewhere to land. I don't hug him. Not yet. He needs to stand on his own two feet through this, even if I'm standing right beside him. "You need to have to deal with the consequences," I continue. "I can go to court with you if you want me to, but you have to decide to control yourself so something like this doesn't happen again."

His throat bobs, marking he swallows. The sun has risen a bit more, lighting up the side of his face. In a way, he looks younger and so much like I did twenty years ago. When I was his age, I had Lacey. We were starting a life together, and I couldn't imagine how much it would kill me to see her out with another guy. I can understand his pain. The ache to comfort him doesn't disappear. "I know it's not fun to take responsibility for this, but I appreciate your honesty. I know you know it's not okay to wreck someone's stuff. I think it's a bigger sign that you need help with your emotions. Whatever happens, we'll deal with it. We can get you some help. You're not alone, okay?"

"I know," he whispers, the words are almost transparent.

Something flickers across his face. It pains to watch him so wounded, but there's a strange steadiness in choosing companionship over lecturing. Finally, I reach out and offer him my arm in a side hug, which he doesn't turn away from. He leans over, and I wrap an arm around him, He's almost eye level with me, but when I hold him, he still feels like the same kid who used to crawl into our bed after nightmares. After patting his arms a few times, I pull away.

"Do you think Mom's going to hate me?"

"She won't," I reassure. "She'll be disappointed, because that's not how she raised you, but she'll still love you. That doesn't change."

He sniffs and hooks my gaze. "I'm sorry."

"I know you are." My throat is thick, as it's healing to talk with Peyton like this. With everything seemingly good on his exterior, I never even assumed he'd have had this internal battle going on, but I feel lucky he's finally opening up. As Lacey would say, "That's the first step. You can't fix your stress by ignoring it." I guess that's maybe a lesson I need to revisit too. "Me too," I say, wholeheartedly. "I'm sorry I didn't notice something was going on with you. I know I need to make more of an effort to have a work and family balance, and trust me, I'm working on it."

"I tried to tell you, but you seemed so depressed about Mom. I didn't think you needed another thing."

My eyebrows bend down. "How'd you know about that, anyway?"

"You're not as good at hiding your emotions as you think you are. It's been painful to watch you fumble this." He nods back toward the cabin. "After months, I figured I'd help you out by getting you two here to at least talk."

I shake my head. All this time I was worried about protecting him from my drama, but he was coming up with a better solution than me.

What a gift this kid is to have.

Maybe I'm realizing it later than I should, but better late than never.

Thirty-Three

LACEY

The front door bursts open, wind rushing in with it. For one dizzy second all I see is snow. Then the voice my heart has been begging for. "Mom," Peyton calls out.

I don't even think. My feet move before my brain catches up, and I race across the room. "Oh, my—Peyton! You seriously scared me."

His cheeks are pink, and my heart flies against my chest wall to see him safe. My arms wrap around him so tight he groans, but I don't care. I press my face to his shoulder, breathing him in.

"Sorry I worried you." Peyton waits for me to pull away, and he steps forward until he plops down on the couch. "Not to make an excuse, but this wasn't my fault. Dad and I had made plans to go fishing. He just forgot."

"Fishing?" My voice cracks, and I quickly clear it. "I was about two minutes from calling the forest rangers."

"It's all my fault." Blake's still by the door, shrugging off his heavy, snow-crusted coat. "He's right. We had plans to get up early and go, but I got all distracted from…"

I blink, catching on to what he's alluding to. "Why didn't you come in and wake Dad up?"

"I don't know." Peyton nods sheepishly. "I just needed to think."

I cross my arms, heart still racing. "Well, that's understandable, but a heads-up about leaving would have been nice. I know you're an adult, and we aren't trying to babysit you, but anyone would be alarmed to wake up to someone missing."

"I get it." He half smiles, but it fades almost instantly. "So, since you're going to ask, I might as well tell you that I got into some trouble," he admits. "It's nothing awful, just something stupid. I already told Dad."

A rare sting of jealousy tugs at my heart as I glance at Blake, who nods slowly while keeping his eyes steady on mine. He's never been one to intercede with the kids' problems. I'm usually the first one they come to. My brows bead together as I think back over the last few months. While I was avoiding Blake, I unintentionally avoided the kids a few times. I guess it might be my fault too. My gaze bounces from Peyton to Blake, and I'm not sure if I should pry. Maybe Peyton isn't comfortable telling me. It might be a boy thing.

Blake speaks before my jealousy has a chance to bloom even more, "Peyton made a mistake and vandalized someone's car. Nobody got hurt, but he got caught."

I exhale. Part of me wants to bombard him with questions, but it had to take a lot of strength for him to admit that. I don't want to shut down the communication now. What if there is more? Oh man, my heart stumbles. I hope there's not more. I cut my gaze to Peyton and offer an empathetic ex-pression. "Life's stressful, honey. It always will be. But hiding things doesn't help. You have to ask for help when you need it."

As the words leave my mouth, I feel Blake's gaze on me. I look over, and our eyes lock.

Ask for help.

It's practically my life's motto. I've said it so many times I'm numb to it. Lately it echoes in my head, louder than it should. Because wasn't that exactly what I stopped doing? Instead, I just gave up. Something stirs low in my chest as his lips slightly part, like he's about to say something, but Peyton yawns, breaking the moment. "Can I take a nap now?" he mumbles.

"Go ahead," I say softly. "We'll talk later."

He drops to his side on the sofa and rolls over, pulling a fleece blanket over him. I fold my arms as my gaze floats over to Paisley. She was quiet this whole time as she watched from the kitchen. I glance back at Blake and surprise myself by saying, "Can we talk somewhere private?"

"Sure," he replies while hiking a thumb over his shoulder. "Should we go out on the porch?"

"Yeah, that sounds nice." I take a step toward the kitchen and say, "Let me make some coffee, and I'll meet you out there."

Blake steps outside, and I go through the motions of heating up a pot of water and throwing some instant coffee into two separate mugs. I don't need coffee. This morning's shenanigans left me jittery enough. I need a moment to collect myself and practice what I want to say to Blake. I didn't think it was possible to have so many emotions at once, but everything, months and years of feelings tumble together.

I'm relieved Peyton is alive.

I can finally breathe. Beneath that relief is a sharp disappointment in myself for missing something so big in his life.

The guilt hits next.

I've spent my entire career telling everyone else to get help, and how bad it is to pretend they're fine. Meanwhile, I kept smiling through my own unraveling until the stress nearly pushed me into a full-blown nervous breakdown.

Hypocrite, party of one, right now making coffee.

And somehow, layered over all that heavy stuff, my skin is still tingling from snuggling with Blake this morning. My brain keeps circling back to one dangerous little thought: maybe I overreacted? Blake and I were always a great team when we actually tried to be. If I'm honest, I can't stop wondering if staying home might have meant I would've noticed Peyton's depression sooner. I wouldn't have admitted it then, but now I can see how I was avoiding Peyton too, because I didn't want him to catch on that I wasn't at the house.

For the first time in months, my chest tenses with a longing for the life I used to have. Not the perfect version I pretended existed, but the imperfect one because even with its messiness, it had a rhythm where things made sense. And then a new thought slips in, bringing a sliver of clarity I've been chasing for weeks. Maybe I never needed to run away from my old life. Maybe I needed to stay and fix the parts that were broken. Because even though it was broken, it was better when my family was whole. As much as I had insisted Blake was the one who needed to learn to appreciate me...I had my own appreciating to do.

"Are you okay, Mom?" Paisley asks as she stands back watching me with a tilted head.

"I don't know what I am right now, but I have a feeling I will be okay," I say with my best even tone. I'm proud I didn't just mutter *I'm fine*. Even though I didn't exactly admit to my issues, I'm making progress. With a cup in each hand, I head outside. Steam curls up from the coffee as I hand Blake his cup. "One black and extra hot, just the way you like it."

He glances over, smiling a little. "Thanks." His fingers brush mine when he takes it. Even through the ceramic heat, I feel the spark. It doesn't feel like my body is betraying me though. Oddly, it feels comfortable. We sit on the old porch swing and listen to it creak as it sways. Neither of us speaks. After a long time, I breathe out a heavy, "I'm sorry."

His head turns slightly, eyes narrowing in quiet surprise. "For what?"

"For all of it." The words are hard to pull out of my chest, but I get through it. "For walking away in a fit. Instead of talking. For making you feel like you weren't enough. You didn't deserve that."

He rests his cup down on the armrest but keeps his hands securely wrapped around the handle like he needs something to hold on to. "I didn't exactly make it easy either."

"No," I say softly, "but still. I should've tried harder before giving up. I kept thinking because I was a counselor, I knew everything and tried everything, but we could have tried counseling together." I take a shaky breath. "The truth is, I was struggling and looking for a quick fix because I lost my mind. I knew better then, and I know better now, but I wasn't thinking straight because I was getting a ton of headaches. When I didn't instantly get better after moving out, I actually finally went to the doctor."

"You did?" His brows lift. "You went to a medical doctor?"

"Yeah. I know. Shocking." I trace a finger around the rim of my mug. "Guess I have a thyroid disorder."

He's quiet for only one quick beat. "Are you going to be okay?"

"Yeah, there's medicine for it." I stare out at the white yard, the morning light catching the snow, lighting up every-thing into thousands of sparkles. "That's the least of my worries though. Seeing Peyton like that," I admit, "scared and ashamed and trying to handle everything on his own. It reminded me I was a terrible role model to the kids as I just shouldered everything myself. It's important not to be ashamed, even when things aren't perfect. Families need to help each other. I hope I'm not too late, but I would like to try again, but this time with help. I'm going to just be honest and say I hate the idea of the hockey team. If you agree to hiring as much help as you can, so it doesn't all land on you, and you still have time for family, and if you can agree to counseling, I'm in. I can't do it alone anymore, but I will try again with help."

"Wow, that's a lot," he says as he blinks back at me. "Of course you aren't too late. It's all I've wanted this whole time, and I'm so sorry. I had no idea you were feeling so badly, but that's my fault because I'm sure you told me. I was so stuck in my own world of trying to support the family. With half the kids in college, I had a lot of pressure to pay those huge bills. It's no excuse, but I'm so sorry I didn't listen."

"I don't think I tried to explain to you what I was feeling. I mostly just nagged you about hockey because it was an easy thing to blame. I'm sure you didn't listen to that part for obvious reasons."

"So, just so I don't mess this up again. You're saying you want to try to work on us." The smile on the tips of his lips is timid, but it doesn't hide his excitement.

"I do."

"Wow, I wasn't expecting that." He rubs his hand over his unshaven face. "I appreciate the second chance, but I have to ask what finally made you change your mind?"

"Just seeing how our kids still need a family, I think. Just because they moved out doesn't mean we don't make sense anymore." I pause and realize how heavy this conversation is. In an effort to lighten it, and to also give him a long overdue compliment, I flirt out, "And maybe you shouldn't have taken your shirt off last night."

He blinks, startled, then laughs. "Well," he says, grinning, "if that's all it took, I would've tried that weeks ago."

I groan and cover my face with my hands, but I'm laughing too. When I lower my hands, he's staring at me with bright eyes. "What?" I ask, still smiling.

Because he's him, he playfully flexes one arm. "Just checking if it's still working."

"Stop." I laugh, shaking my head, but when he leans closer, the air shifts. The teasing fades into something deeper.

"What can I do," he asks softly, "to be a better husband?"

My heart stumbles. There are a hundred things I could say. A thousand promises we've both broken and forgiven. But at this moment, none of them matter.

"Just hold me," I whisper. That's all it takes for his arms to wrap around me, and I let out an even breath as the lump in my throat smooths and my breathing eases.

If anyone ever asks me how to ruin a perfectly good emotional breakthrough, I'll tell them: let Blake make breakfast.

To be fair, we had proper warning when he almost burned the cabin down last night. We should have bolted the doors to the cabinets, so he had nothing to cook with. He insisted he's turning a new leaf and wants to help with all the domestic stuff to be more present. I liked the sound of that and stood back when he took charge with a bowl and a whisk, stirring up pancake mix while heating a pan of oil on the stove. He looks like he knows what he's doing as he ladles pancakes into the pan and then turns to open the fridge.

It's making me nervous, he's so fast to turn his back to the stove. I keep an eye on the pan from the antique—as it came with the cabin—kitchen table. Part of me is hoping he has a knack for cooking. I mean, all these years of marriage, and I never had any help in the kitchen. I would adore a breakfast chef. Yet I'm leery as I pretend to nurse my coffee. It's not long before I smell something burning. "Uh, Blake?" I state as calmly as I can while setting my mug down. My legs itch to fly to the stove, but again, the counselor in me is telling me we can coach our way through this.

He's got his head in the fridge, digging around for something, and either doesn't hear me or is concentrating so hard on finding the bacon, he can't reply.

Whoosh!

Meep. Meep. Meep.

A puff of a flame taking flight in the pan swirls through the air, and it's immediately followed by the unmistakable screech of the smoke alarm. Apparently, he left a corner of a dish towel a little too close to the pan.

No longer waiting for him to take control, I bolt up, waving my arms to move the smoke out while Blake snatches the smoking dish towel out of the flaming pan, and tosses it into the sink. "Go sit outside!" he shouts over the shrill beep as he grabs the water sprayer, dousing the rag. "I've got this under control!"

Coughing out a laugh, I can barely breathe. Or maybe it's the smoke that's taking my breath? Either way, I'm not staying around here to get smoked out. I slide my foot toward the door, and tease on the way out, "Those are going to be *charcoal pancakes*!"

He glares at me over his shoulder, but his lips twitch. "They're extra crispy, and it's good for detox."

"Detox!" I giggle. "Because nobody will eat them." Peyton rushes up behind me, stretches tall, and punches the button on the alarm until blessed silence fills the kitchen.

"Dad." His nose wrinkles as he ducks, dodging the smoke. "That smells awful."

Blake grabs the pan with an oven mitt, marches out the door, and dumps the smoking remains into the snow. When he returns, he grumbles something I can't make out and drops the ruined pan in the sink. I'm still laughing, as I can't believe we're back in a smoke-filled cabin. "Hey, I used to be smooth," he says, returning to the stove as we both know he's not giving up now. He's stubborn, and he'll make breakfast even if he needs a hazmat suit.

"Oh really?" I arch a brow. "When?"

"Don't you remember prom? You couldn't keep your eyes off me."

Heat blooms on my cheeks. I hate he remembers details like that, because—well, because it makes me gooey inside. So, no, maybe I don't hate that he remembers it, but it makes me swallow hard. "That was over two decades ago."

He smirks. "It worked, didn't it?"

I roll my eyes. "Questionable."

"*Dad*," Paisley moans as she climbs down from the loft and heads straight to the coat hook, where she quickly cloaks herself in an overcoat. "Are we seriously going to have to sit on the porch again? It's freezing out there." Peyton steps forward with her, grabs his coat off the wall hook and throws it on before passing through the door, where they take their seats on the porch.

I slip in behind Blake, shoving him lightly, trying not to grin too wide. "Next time it's your turn to cook, promise you order in."

"Deal." He playfully narrows his eyes.

I don't exactly know what we're doing this morning. It's fun to have the kids around. It's a rhythm I've missed. Maybe everything I've missed. Part of me yearns for my other two boys to be here too, but I'm grateful for the family who is here with me now, especially for Blake. Somehow, through all the mess, he's managed to be the glue I desperately tried to remove when I didn't see how much I needed it.

By afternoon, the cabin smells like cocoa and only light woodsmoke appropriately coming from the fireplace and not the house burning down. Outside, snow falls in thick hushes, piling into the driveway so much that I don't think I could leave now if I tried. We'll need to wait for the plow to come. I don't mind.

Inside, the four of us have somehow fallen into a rhythm that feels like old times. Paisley's got a favorite puzzle of a snowy mountain village scene spread across the dining table, and Peyton's half-watching a hockey game on mute. Blake's rummaging through the kitchen drawers, pretending he knows where everything is, as he's convinced me to let him make chili. I keep my eyes on him, making sure he doesn't dare touch the stove again. We settled on the crockpot for this round.

"Mom," Paisley says while she picks up the puzzle box and frowns. "Seriously, this is the hardest puzzle ever. Everything is white. Who buys a puzzle like this?"

"Your grandmother," I groan with agreement as that puzzle hurts my brain. "She believed in brain exercises and doing hard things."

"It's so cruel," she mutters, as Blake wanders over and squints down at the table.

"Oh, I see where that one goes," he says confidently, sliding in beside her, picking up a piece and positioning it in the bottom corner.

"Do you?" Paisley challenges. "Because that's literally the sky, and that's not where it goes."

He shoots a mock glare. "I played pro hockey. I can handle a puzzle."

"Not the same thing." Peyton perks up from his spot on the couch, his gaze cutting to the puzzle too.

"Not exactly the same thing, but it's mind endurance," Blake fires back. I don't miss that his thumb hovers over his piece, as he's visibly trying to force it to fit into a spot it shouldn't.

"No cheating, Blake." I warn as I sip my cocoa.

Blake tosses his hands up. "Okay, fine, maybe I don't see where it goes."

I can't help but laugh. "Admitting defeat already?"

He straightens, feigning indignation. "It's not defeat. It's redirection." His fingers slide the piece to the sky where he easily attaches it to one of the few open sky places. Not one to back down from anything that can be made into a competition, Peyton gets up from the couch and joins the other two at the table. I'm not going to be left out, so I slide my chair over, and start taking score.

For the next hour, the four of us are lost in the puzzle. There's laughter and memories being recalled, a few too many accusations of cheating and most of all, that easy rhythm we used to have before everything cracked apart. At one point Blake leans back, laughing so hard he has to wipe his eyes.

Something inside me aches.

I fill in another piece of the puzzle to what was actually bothering me this whole time. Yes, part of it was my thyroid, and part of it was my marriage. Another piece was possibly the stress of my job, but a bigger piece was the overwhelming loneliness I felt from being an empty nester. I think deep down, I was expecting Blake to fill all that emptiness. When he didn't, I resented him even more. It's funny how it all makes sense now. "Okay," I say when I push the last piece in the puzzle and glance around. "It's all done."

Blake nudges my knee with his. "Good. Because my famous chili should be done. I have to throw some corn bread in the oven to warm it up."

"Oh no you're not!" I jump up and pretend to block him. "You are never touching the stove or oven or anything flammable again."

The kids groan in unison, but they're smiling. Blake shoots up from his chair, racing over to the kitchen while dramatically pushing up his sleeves. "I got it all covered," he calls over his shoulder, but I'm right on his heels.

"If you're going to cook," I refute, "I'm helping. I'm not spending another minute on that porch."

His eyes level with mine as a smile cracks wide on his face. "I'd love to cook with you."

I smile back at him, knowing things are changing between us. It's not back to normal, but what is normal anyway? In a twenty-five year plus relationship, you go through phases. This is the start of a new phase. I'm not sure what it is exactly, but I don't feel anger toward him anymore. If anything, I feel grateful that he's stuck by me this long. So, maybe I'm entering my acceptance phase finally. Not accepting we are separated, but more so agree to live a life together, knowing nothing about it will be perfect. There will be pain. There will be so many disappointments, but also, there will be laughter and so much love. I just have to decide not to ever give up because if I had... I flick a glance back at the kids still sitting at the table, and my heart swells. If I'd have given up last summer when I wanted to, I'd have missed out on today, and many more amazing days like this.

That's not something I'm willing to do.

Thirty-Four

Blake

Credits roll, and the living room is full of that sleepy quiet that comes after too much food and a familiar movie. Paisley's half asleep with her head against the couch armrest, and Peyton's snoring softly in the recliner.

Lacey softly laughs beside me. "I guess you can sleep through the movie when you've seen it before."

"They've seen *Mighty Ducks* at least ten times," I say, grinning.

"I'd say more like fifty." She stands and stretches, her sweater lifting just enough for me to see the faint curve of her back. Then without saying anything, she turns toward the hallway, and I follow. The floor creaks under our feet, but it's comforting. Everything about the cabin feels softer tonight. Like it's remembering for us, so we finally remember who we are. When we reach the bedroom, she pauses in the doorway and looks at the bed. She stands there, biting her lip, a faint blush rising. "Well, here we are again."

"Yeah," I say, my voice low. I glance down at it, then back up at her. "I can take the floor."

She tilts her head, eyes glinting at me. "Well, you could if you really want or"—her voice drops just a little, playful—"you could take your shirt off again and get your spot back."

I choke out a laugh, but inside my heart flutters hard against my rib cage. The fact she's allowing me into our bed is a huge step that I don't take for granted. "That's all it takes, huh?"

She shrugs as her lips twitch. "Apparently."

So, I do it. I grab the hem of my T-shirt, yank it over my head, and toss it toward the chair like it's some kind of joke.

It's not though.

Not really.

But sort of is when I playfully flex in her direction.

She's still laughing when she climbs into bed, shaking her head. "You're ridiculous."

"Maybe," I say, sliding under the covers beside her. "But I got my spot back."

"That you did." She sighs and rolls over on her side. I stretch out, pulling the blanket flat over us, and lie in the dark. Except for the moonlight slipping through the blinds, I can't see anything. My fingers twitch as I resist the urge to hold her. I don't want to make her uncomfortable. The gentleman in me tells me to wait for her to make the first move. Her breathing slows beside me into the comforting tempo I used to fall asleep to every night. After a while, she whispers, "They're good kids, huh?"

"The best," I whisper back. "We did something right."

She turns her head. Even in the dark, I can feel her eyes on me. "Yeah. I think Peyton really needed this time. He was laughing a lot more today than I've seen him laugh in forever. Hopefully, he's on the mend."

The curve of her cheek in the pale light causes my breath to hitch in the back of my throat. It's the kind of beauty that's always had a chokehold on me. At this point, I'd do anything to be able to make this sleeping arrangement permanent again. "It's been everything," I admit quietly. "Being here with you."

Her throat moves as she swallows. "Yeah. It felt good to me too."

I listen to the silence. We don't say *I miss you*. We don't say *I'm sorry*. We just lie side by side, and that speaks the loudest anything has ever to me.

After a long moment, she exhales, and in a voice barely a whisper says, "Goodnight."

"Goodnight," I say back, though I don't close my eyes right away. Because lying here, close enough to feel the warmth of her arm brushing mine, I feel home.

Thirty-Five

LACEY

I drift in and out of the lightest sleep, as my mind is reeling. No matter which way I scoot on this lumpy, old mattress, I'm met with a broken spring. It's playing Whack-a-Mole with my hip. I surprisingly don't startle when Blake's hand finds the small of my back. For years I told myself I didn't need this anymore. That we were too busy, too tired, too far gone. But right now, with his chin resting lightly on my hair, I realize how much I've missed being held like this.

"Are you comfortable?" he asks.

"Not really, but it's not you. It's this bed." I sigh heavily as I tug on my pillow again. "Are you comfortable?

"More than I've ever been." He chuckles lightly, and it sends a shiver straight down my spine.

I tilt my head to look up at him. Suddenly we're face-to-face, and his eyes search mine. I don't turn away. I let him see me. Familiar yearning for a kiss from him stirs in my heart, but I don't dare make a move. Part of me feels like maybe I don't deserve it after everything I put him through these last months. He holds my gaze and grins, brushing his thumb across my cheek while he whispers, "You're beautiful."

Heat rushes up my neck. After over twenty-five years of marriage, you'd think those words would lose their power, but they don't.

Not when he says them like that.

Not with all the years of raising babies and not feeling pretty.

A compliment feels hard earned. It's also enough of an invitation for me to risk resting my head on his chest, and he doesn't waste a moment to wrap his arm all the way around me. Goosebumps spiral up my arm, causing a sigh to slip from my lips. I don't think I could sleep now if I ate a bottle of melatonin. Giving up on the idea of rest, I invite him into my memories, "Do you remember the night we walked down to the beach at two in the morning?"

I don't see it, but I can feel him smile against my hair. "Yeah, that was when you were pregnant with Paul, and you had insomnia. You kept me up all night, every night, because you couldn't stop moving around...or peeing."

"He literally slept on my bladder." I laugh softly, closing my eyes. "I haven't thought about that in years."

"That's the problem," he murmurs. "We stopped remembering the good things."

"I'm not sure if the constant peeing is a good thing," I joke, but still sit in the memory. Instead of sadness, a spark of hope flutters right as his hand starts to stroke down my arm.

"Let's promise to always make time for each other."

My throat tightens. Part of me feels like he's only saying that now because he can't sneak off to work while we're stranded out here, but I don't want to be bitter anymore. Resistance feels pointless now. Blake's a good man. He's always been faithful, and I just need things—us—to feel whole again, and I always felt the best when I had my family together.

My family is worth trying to fix my marriage again.

They are worth trying a million times.

What Blake and I had—correction have—is worth trying for a lifetime. "Okay," I say softly, but I don't crave anymore conversation. It's like my body needs to just soak up Blake's warmth. It's the most healing thing I've done. Months of stress melt away, relaxing me farther into his embrace. After a while, I drift to sleep, knowing nothing is perfect but nothing is wrong either. It's just all a part of life.

And that is the biggest win of all.

I wake up to my nose tickling.

The smell of something warm and *burning!*

Jolting upright, my eyes snap open. To my horror I find the plaid comforter pulled back on Blake's side and the sheets are empty!

I know everything I need to know.

Blake is cooking—or rather burning the kitchen down. I stumble out of bed, narrowly missing hooking my toe on the edge of the bedpost. So glad that didn't happen because I have no time for a stubbed toe. I yank my robe from the back of the door, throw it over my flannel night shirt, and race out the door. Just two steps down the dimly lit hall, I start choking on smoke. Cold drafts of air meet my bare toes.

Blake flies in from the porch carrying another smoking pot right to the sink. His brows are lowered in defeat, but I can't help but laugh. Peyton rolls over on the couch, yelling, "Dad! Stop trying to kill us!"

Paisley flies down the stairs and stops when she sees everything is mostly under control. We all take turns exchanging looks before I say, "I'll make some coffee and meet you all on the porch."

"Deal!" Everyone cheers in unison. Peyton wraps his blanket around him as he sleepily pulls himself from the couch and drags his feet toward the door. I'm laughing because as chaotic as it is, it's exactly what my mama heart needs. Another little pocket of my heart is healing, planting a grin on my face.

I grab my coat, throw it over my robe, not caring how ridiculous I must look. Outside, the lightest little fairy dust snow glitters under a pale sun, and I squint as I fight my eyes from watering. The kids plop on the wooden rocking chairs. I take a spot on the porch swing, sitting far enough to one side to purposely leave room for Blake. When he finally joins us, just a minute later, he's put on his boots and heavy coat, and he goes right to the railing that's covered in fresh snow. I catch him scooping up the perfect snowball amount, and I shout, "Don't you dare."

Too late.

The snowball arcs through the air and splats in my lap.

My mouth drops open, and I scream.

The next thing I know, I'm ducking behind a chair while Peyton chucks a snowball the size of a grapefruit at my head. It explodes, showering me with icy shrapnel. I don't even care that I'm so cold my extremities tremble. We chase each other, all laughing like maniacs, until I finally slip on the slick ice near the steps. Reflex takes over, and I grapple for something to break my fall, pulling on Blake's arm. We both tumble down the steps, landing on our butts in a heap of snow. "Ouch," I cry out as I moan and grab my back.

Blake's already rebounded to his feet and reaches down, brushing snowflakes from my hair. And something clicks.

This is it.

This is us.

Not the years of fighting.

Not the silence.

Just two idiots in the snow, still stupidly doing life together, and it feels good.

My teeth chatter by the time Blake grabs my hand and yanks me up with so much force I fall into him. Okay, maybe I helped fall into him a little. He takes advantage of my nearness and wraps his arms all the way around me, freezing me into place. My eyes pace around his face, and I feel nothing but safe. "Okay," I say after a beat, "you've redeemed yourself."

"Good." His lips slide into the cockiest grin he has. "Because if this didn't work, I was going to bury you in the snow."

I laugh, taking his hand into mine as I straighten to balance on my feet again, and we walk back up the stairs. It's just two steps, but it feels like we conquered so much more than that.

Two steps.

And two hearts, finally beating as one again.

Thirty-Six

Blake

Later that morning, Lacey and I cuddle on the couch, sharing a blanket. The fire in the fireplace—that she started but I'm not holding a grudge about—is crackling low. She's got her feet tucked under her, a mug of tea in hand, and I swear she looks younger. Not in a superficial way. There's a light in her eyes I haven't seen in too long. I watch her sip. Before I can stop myself, I blurt, "I'm sorry about my loud chewing."

Her brows lift. "The what?"

"You said I chewed really loud," I repeat, heat creeping up my neck. "You know when you got mad and left."

She blinks and lets out a laugh, setting her mug down. "Are you seriously apologizing for something I complained about?"

"Yes." I run a hand through my hair, sheepish. "I never really listened when you asked me to chew with my mouth closed. It was like my thing to eat really fast and in front of the TV. I thought you should just learn to live with it. Now I see that's not fair. It was really gross. So yeah, I'm sorry."

She stares at me like I just sprouted a second head. Her lips curl into this smile that makes my chest ache. "You know what? I actually kind of missed it."

"Missed it?" I choke out.

She shrugs, as her hand slides onto my lap, spiraling goose-bumps over the trail until her fingers slip into mine, and she gently squeezes my hand. "It was irritating, sure. But it was you. And I found out the hard way that things are really quiet by myself. Even your chewing has a way of making a place feel like home."

Something in me breaks open at that. I turn my palm, bringing her fingers up to my lips, and kiss them gently, closing my eyes at the way her skin smells as it always does. The softest hint of vanilla. When I open my eyes, I level my gaze with hers and rasp, "Well, I don't want us to have to miss each other like that ever again."

Her eyes soften, and she leans her head on my shoulder. "Okay. Then no more missing."

I inch closer. When she doesn't pull away, I kiss the top of her head and hold her tighter.

It's not some grand gesture.

I was never good at that anyway.

It's just us, sharing a tattered blanket that's warmed three generations of our family. I'm not in a rush to push this reunion, because I have hope that if we do it right, we have a long future ahead of us.

After a moment, Peyton returns from using the bathroom and stares at us. "Don't you think we should get back on the road? It's a long drive."

I know exactly what time it is, and he's right. The weekend is winding down, and Monday is back to work. I don't want to move as I have everything I need right here. Having another idea, Lacey stands, squeezing my hand before she yanks me up after her, and says, "Let's go home."

Questions sound alarms in my heart. Is this really the moment I've been praying for? Is she really coming home, home to our house?

I can't stop staring, and my mouth doesn't work. I'm sure there's a catch, but I don't ask for details. I'm happy to go back home. My heart slams against my chest, as I'm suddenly fearful everything will go back to the way it was. I want things to stay like this with her and us.

"What?" she asks.

"Nothing." I shake my head, as my guts twists, begging for clarification. "Just you..." I trail off, struggling to find the words. "This sort of feels like home. You and me, and I just don't want to lose it when we go back."

Her expression softens. "Yeah. It does."

The silence between us is charged in a good way. I want to kiss her, but I hesitate. She must see something because she solves that problem by leaning over like it's the most natural thing in the world, tilting her head up, and planting her lips on mine.

Wowzers!

I didn't even know that word was in my vocabulary, but the electricity in her lips is hotter than when we were newlyweds. My whole body lights up, and I kiss her back as my hand slides around her back. I've missed this.

And then—

"AHEM."

We jerk apart like guilty teenagers. Paisley stands on the bottom step, smirking like she's caught us committing a crime. "You two are gross," she declares. "But also, I'm kind of glad to see that, because to be honest, I was a little worried about you."

Beaming with pride, I wave her off. "Go get your stuff together. We're leaving soon."

She pivots, heading back up to her loft, muttering about how she "didn't need that mental image." When she's no longer visible, I can't help it, and I lean in and steal another kiss from Lacey's waiting lips. I don't care if the kids see us. No, that's not right. I want the kids to see us happy and in a loving relationship.

I've gone so long without this woman. I have some serious lost time to make up for. I draw her closer to me, and she melts into my arms, as she doesn't seem to mind either.

Epilogue

I stare at the little white stick on the bathroom counter like it's a live grenade. My stomach flips, my hands shake, and I swear I can hear the tick of the wall clock three rooms away.

This is ridiculous.

I'm forty-eight years old.

Forty-eight.

Women like me don't get pregnant.

We get hot flashes.

We get reading glasses.

We don't grow humans.

And yet.

I bite my lip, pacing in my robe. I only bought the test because my period was late. Which, let's face it, happens when you're this age. But the nagging voice in the back of my head wouldn't quit. The same voice that's been whispering every time I yawn at three in the afternoon, or when I feel queasy in the mornings, or when my boobs are sore in a way that feels entirely too familiar. With two fingers, I pinch it off the counter. My eyes swell huge.

Two PINK lines.

Laughter bursts out a little too high-pitched to pass for joy. "Oh my!" I grab the counter for balance, as my knees threaten mutiny. My heart's pounding like I sprinted a mile.

A baby.

At forty-eight.

I should be crying or something appropriately dramatic. Instead, all I can do is laugh, cover my mouth with my hand, because if I don't, I might scream.

Blake and I have just gotten our marriage back on track. We've been rediscovering each other in ways that make me feel like a teenager sneaking kisses again. We were finally good about "just us" time. And now, "Surprise," I whisper to the stick. I pace out of the bathroom and flop onto my neatly made bed, all the while my head spins. I can practically see my kids' faces when they find out. But beneath the disbelief, there's a warmth blooming in my chest.

Hope.

Grabbing the square throw pillow from the pile of perfectly aligned pillows, I press it over my face, laughing until tears sting my eyes.

Life just refuses to be boring.

Maybe that's not such a bad thing.

Epilogue

Blake

I'm toweling sweat off my shoulders after my morning work-out when Lacey comes flying into the gym. It's not her usual stop on the way to work, but we've both been taking extra time to include each other in our days. I'm not totally surprised to see her here. She's dressed in her school clothes, but I halt on my heel when I see how wide her eyes are. "Babe?" I drop the towel, instantly on alert. "What happened?"

She opens her mouth, closes it, and inhales a deep breath. "Okay, don't freak out."

"Pretty sure you just guaranteed I'm going to freak out."

She bites her lip, pulls something from her purse, and holds it out—a little white stick.

It takes me a second.

It's been a long time since I've had to see one of these. When my brain catches up, my mouth goes dry, and I choke out, "Wait. Is that—"

"Positive," she blurts out, the word tumbling fast. "I'm pregnant. At least, I think so. I haven't seen a doctor yet, but I've never had a false positive."

I blink at her.

Then at the stick.

Then back at her.

"Blake, say something, you're scaring me." She pulls the stick back in front of her, holding it in the center of her body like she's protecting it.

This is so far beyond what I ever expected. "You are pregnant?" I grin like an idiot as a laugh leaks out of my mouth. "You're kidding."

She crosses her arms, playfully scowling. "I knew you'd laugh. This is serious!"

Planting both feet firmly in front of her, I scan her entire face for a twist that this is a joke. All she has is her dead-serious eyes, and my gut tugs tight, and I whisper, "You're not kidding?"

"No." She pushes her chin forward. "This is for real."

I blink once.

Then again as my heart begins to pump harder.

I can no longer stand still, and I lunge forward, cupping her face, kissing her forehead. "This is incredible! I mean, we thought that chapter was closed, right? But look at us overachievers."

Her eyes shine up at me in a way that makes me feel like we are the only two people on the planet. "You're not mad?"

"Mad? Lacey, I never even thought this might be a possibility, but after the last few months without you, this is the best news ever." I kiss her on the lips now, letting my lips linger with all the joy overflowing. I break it off and blurt, "I couldn't be happier."

Her laugh breaks on a sob, tugging on my heart. I get this is a lot harder for her to deal with than me. It's her body that will be in charge of growing our baby, and it's a lot to take on at her age, but I'm here for it. I'm here for her. I'm here for the baby. I pull her into my chest, and she melts into my embrace. And then, because it's us, the serious moment shifts. I tilt her chin, brush my thumb across her lips, and say, "Also, for the record, this proves I've still got it."

She smacks my shoulder, laughing, and I scoop her up like I used to when we were first married, spinning her until she squeals.

A baby.

At almost fifty.

Life is about to get wild again.
And honestly?
I'm all in.

Epilogue

Lacey

We invited all four of the kids over for a family dinner. We aren't even at the table yet, and Paisley's whispering to me in the kitchen, "You're not divorcing, are you?"

"No," I'm quick to rebut. "It's not like that, at all."

"Well, can you just tell us what's going on, because it's all over your face that something is wrong, and I can't wait."

"I mean, I guess I can tell you." My gaze slides across the room, meeting Blake's as he's at the table. He doesn't say anything but gives me a silent nod.

Okay. Here goes nothing.

"So," I begin, my voice wobbling as I do my best to project it so the boys at the table can hear too. "We, uh, have some news."

Four pairs of eyes lock on me.

Blake grins and holds an arm out to me, until I walk over and join him at his side. Not one of the kids makes the tiniest sound. I open my mouth and release the words I've rehearsed. "You're going to be big brothers again." I shift my gaze to Paisley, my sweet baby girl, who isn't the baby anymore, and add, "You're going to be a big sister."

Paul chokes on his water.

Peyton stares blankly.

Paisley mutters, "What the actual—"

"You're kidding, right?" Preston says in a rather demanding tone.

"Nope," Blake says cheerfully as he pulls me closer, wrapping his hand around my back. "Dead serious."

"You're lying," Paisley groans, burying her face in her hands. "You're like ancient."

"Excuse me?" I protest. "Forty-eight is not ancient."

"It is for a uterus!" she fires back, and the boys collapse in laughter.

"Dad, you're going to be seventy at graduation," Paul blurts out.

I start laughing but then Preston gives me a suspicious side-eye. "Well, I guess this confirms we don't have to worry about you two divorcing anymore. Here I thought you might still be fighting. At least you two are obviously doing okay."

Heat floods my cheeks as it's so oddly embarrassing to have to tell grown kids what you've been up to with your husband. "Oh, shut up." I shake my head and laugh lightly as I take a moment to look at each one of my four beautiful children. It's been the joy of my life to be their mom. I never once thought I'd get a chance to do it again.

But here I am.

Blake smiles down, and I wink back.

Our family's about to get bigger.

Nothing else has ever felt more right.

Bonus Epilogue

About nine months later

"All right, Piper." I pace with my one-month baby girl like a man in baby boot camp. "For the record, I've faced down a lot tougher crowds than you. I once played through a dislocated shoulder in front of twenty thousand fans. So, you don't scare me."

Piper responds with an ear-splitting shriek that makes me wince. "Fine. You win. Your mom was right. You're the boss here." My phone buzzes on the side table. I reach for it, careful not to jostle the baby. A text alert flashes across the screen from one of my old contacts in the league: Coach Carlson, who is Bill's head coach.

Big news. Call me ASAP.

My gut tightens as I quickly swipe, pressing the phone to my ear. "Hey. What's going on?" I whisper, hoping not to set off the Piper alarm.

"It's Bill Baker. Word just dropped that he's forced to sell Granite Ice."

"Sell the team?" I repeat, glancing down at Piper who is suspiciously quiet now, staring up with big blue eyes.

"That's right," he confirms. "They're already lining up buyers. It's getting competitive. I thought I'd give you a heads-up. I know you're originally from Mapleton. I think you need to consider getting in the bidding."

My mind slams into race mode. For years, I've been living under the shadow of Bill—his ex-friend, his rival. And now Bill is about to lose his precious hockey team.

And I have the chance to step in.

I'd be the winner.

I'd have his team, his girl, and his stepson.

There's nothing more I'd ever want.

But I shouldn't.

I have enough on my plate right now.

Or should I say chest? I press a kiss to the baby's head, my heart thumping. I glance around the living room. An assortment of pink blankets is tossed over the couch, a swing tucked near the coffee table, and a scatter of clean laundry trails the length of the couch. A diaper bag slouches open on my favorite recliner because that's the only thing that has time to sit anymore. It still looks like a living room, technically—but only in the way a battlefield still counts as a field. Yeah, Lacey and I have our hands full. "I really shouldn't. We just had a baby—"

"If you walk away," Coach cuts in, "someone else is going to thank you for it later. Think about it. This is Mapleton. Your hometown for both you and your wife."

A vision of the headline, "Anton Saves Mapleton Team" flashes through my head. I've always been a sucker for the headlines. What that would do to Bill. A competitive spiral grows in my chest, and I blurt out, "Tell them to put my name on the list," I say. "I want that team."

"I knew you would." Coach laughs.

As the call ends, I let out a long breath, resting my cheek against Piper's' soft hair. "See that, Piper? Daddy has all the luck."

She squirms a little, but I bounce her the way all my older kids liked to bounce. Shocked I still remember this baby trick, I grin wider, as I confide in her, "Yeah, I know. Mom's going to kill me when she finds out."

The bouncing is making her eyes drift down, and she miraculously curls into my chest and falls asleep. That's a win for me. A hard-earned one too since she hasn't been the best sleeper. I take advantage of the moment and hurry back to her room, placing her into her crib. Another miracle happens and she doesn't stir, and I back away as quietly as I can. With urgency, I race to the next room over and find Lacey's halfway asleep when I crawl into bed next to her.

"Hey," she says sleepily. "Is she okay?"

"Sleeping like an angel," I say, then take a moment to brag. "Because of me. I'm basically a baby whisperer now."

She smiles with her eyes closed. Clearly, she wants to sleep, but I must tell her my plan. There can't be any secrets between us ever, and I don't ever want her to doubt me again. I clear my throat. "So, listen. You might hear some things soon, but I want you to hear it from me first."

Her eyes pop open like they are spring loaded. "That's never a good sentence."

"Depends on how you look at it," I start. "Apparently Bill's being forced to sell Granite Ice. And I, well, I might have said I'm throwing my hat in the ring to be the next owner. I'm making a bid."

"You're what—" she cuts herself off, pressing her palm to her forehead. "You own a team, and a gym, and a media company. You have a newborn. When exactly are you planning to run that team?"

I chuckle as I lean closer to her and wrap an arm around her. "See, I knew you'd take it well."

"This isn't well!" she hisses at me as her whole body goes stiff from my touch. "This is exactly what we agreed not to do. We are supposed to make decisions together now. This is insane!"

"It's not insane," I counter. "It's strategic. Bill's out. His team's floundering. As much as I am not a fan of his, it's Mapleton, a town we both love. It means a lot to the community, and I know I can save it."

She pinches the bridge of her nose while her eyes close too tight, every last beautiful crow's foot in the corners of her eyes creases. "I just...I don't know if this is about an investment or beating Bill."

Silence stretches for a moment as I consider her honest question. Then I lower my voice. "It's both," I admit. "But mostly? It's about proving to myself I can do it."

"Blake," she whispers, softer now. "You don't need to prove anything. You're more than enough."

"I know," I say. "But I need it for me, and don't worry. I have a plan where it won't take any more time away from our family. In fact, it might actually give me more time with you."

Finally, she sighs. It's not her happy sigh, but it's also not her upset one either. "Fine," she mutters. "But when people ask why I have worry lines, I'm sending them straight to you."

"Deal." I lean over and kiss her forehead, and she seems already to be drifting to sleep. I've never felt happier.

Bonus Epilogue

A Month Later

It's been years since I've been back in Mapleton, and it makes
sense the first place I stop is the old park, where I learned
to skate. Only, I'm not here to skate. It's a different kind of
meetup. My eyes narrow as I spot the person I came to see.

"Well, well," Bill taunts. "I don't believe it. Did you come
to gloat?"

My shoulders tense, and I resist the urge to roll them like
I used to before a fight. I'm not here to trade punches. "I'm

not here to brag," I say evenly. "I'm here to talk about Granite Ice."

Bill's laugh is sharp. "My team is not your business."

"Yeah, I hear it's not going to be yours for much longer," I reply. "I tried to bid on it, but the league denied it, since I already have ownership in a team. They said it's a conflict."

Silence stretches between us before I go on, "I'm the only one who tried to bid on the team, Bill. Nobody else wants it, because the stats are terrible, but I know I can do this. Not to rub it in your face or anything. Maybe at first when I heard about this, I thought that would be fun, but the more I thought about it, the team's right here in Mapleton, and Mapleton is where I grew up and fell in love with hockey. I feel like I can pay it back a little by helping you out."

An unrecognizable emotion flicks across Bill's face. He's quiet as I step forward and say the words I practiced all morning on the drive here, "You know, I've been waiting to talk to you for twenty-five years. And yeah, maybe I made some bad calls. Maybe you did things you shouldn't have. But the truth is..." I let out a long breath. "The truth is, I let it eat me alive. I let it take more from me than you ever could. I'm letting it go finally."

Bill shifts his gaze, looking away.

For once, the smugness is gone.

Bill's jaw slides forward, like he wants to spit venom. "Why are you telling me this if the league didn't approve it?"

Shifting my weight from one leg to the other, I'm not as nervous as I thought I'd be. I'm calm. Like everything we've been through has been leading us to this moment. "I think we can come up with a plan to save it together."

His eyes narrow but he doesn't pause. "What are you thinking?"

"Well, I'm thinking about forming a trust with Noah and Paisley as owners. That way you can still stay involved, unofficially. Paisley has worked for me before, and she's smart, and Noah, you've seen him play. He's fast, but he struggles with stickhandling. As he ages, he's going to get swallowed up by the new recruits who don't have that weakness. But he's got more heart than anyone I know. Under our mentorship, I think the two of them can turn that team around.

"What about Arctic Force?" He leans in just a bit. "That makes you and Paisley rivals. Do you really want that?"

"I thought about that, and I don't think it makes us rivals," I say slowly as I pondered every possible way this scenario might go. I mean, I could let Granite Ice dissolve because they are terrible. However, as much as I hate to admit it, I love that my hometown has a hockey team. There's something special about Mapleton. "I'm going to be a silent member behind the trust, but I'll be rooting for our kids for sure. I actually think it will make us more partners than we've ever been."

"Are you saying you are willing to put our differences aside to save Granite Ice?" Bill's voice is gruff as if in disbelief.

"I know it sounds crazy, because we've been so competitive all these years, but our kids are together now. Unless we want the loneliest holidays for the next thirty years, we have to find a way to get along." I stop to think about all the ways my life has changed in the last few years. After coming so close to losing Lacey, and her forgiving me when I really didn't deserve it, I feel like I can forgive too. It's the biggest feeling of relief to let out an easy breath and say, "Yeah, for the sake of our families, I'm in if you are."

Bill extends his hand, offering a handshake. It's a moment of time that freezes. Never did I ever think I'd touch his snakeskin again. I'm not one-hundred-percent certain this is a good idea. With Bill, there are always surprises, but I trust Paisley. For her, I grip his hand as he says, "You have yourself a partner."

"Speaking of partner." My gaze shifts over my shoulder, and something changes in my chest instantly. A slow, knowing smirk pulls at my mouth. I don't say anything right away, as I wait for Bill to notice Lacey's here, and has been here the whole time. After she had the baby, she decided to take a break from counseling to have more time to focus on just the family. Now, we spend a good portion of our days doing life together. "You remember Lacey," I add, my chest puffing with pride. "My wife." Obviously, he remembers her. It's more than an introduction. It's a silent message to Bill. I wave her over, "Honey, did you have any questions?"

He glances back, just enough to confirm what he already knows. Sidestepping to make room for her, she meets me shoulder to shoulder. Exactly where she belongs. It's been a lot of years coming, to face Bill together, but I've never been taller. "Morning, Bill," she says with ease. "Nice to see you."

"It's good to see you both, and still together after all of these years." Bill offers a nod toward Lacey.

My hand finds Lacey's lower back. "Yeah," I say, smiling at her with something grounded. "It's amazing how fast life goes by, but it turned out better than I expected. We actually just had our fifth child. A beautiful, healthy baby girl, who looks just like her mother." Lacey squeezes my arm. Maybe it's her subtle way to get me to stop talking, but it feels more like she's supporting me, and I can't stop gushing. "It hasn't all been easy, but it's good."

Bill's expression stays neutral, but his eyes soften. "I'm glad to hear that. You have a beautiful family."

I tip my head toward Lacey. "I owe it all to Lacey." Shifting my weight from one leg to the other, I do my best to pay back his compliment. "Yeah. I've been getting to know your stepson. Noah. He's got some wheels. That's for sure. Very fast, and it looks like Paisley's going to keep him around for a while. He's good to her. I'd never have guessed my daughter would end up with someone related to you, but after seeing the two of them together, I'm grateful for that too."

Lacey's head jerks back a little, as if she's as shocked as I am I said something so nice to Bill's face. As if I also need a little more convincing, I add, "You know what, Bill. It feels good to finally put the past where it belongs."

He's quick to nod with his approval. "I couldn't agree more. Maybe after all these years we finally matured."

We all laugh at that with Lacey being the loudest, and inserting, "Boy, I hope so."

"Well, hate to cut this short," I say. "We have a baby to get back too. We left Preston on baby duty, and he's probably about at his limit."

"Yeah, I have a meeting to get to as well." Bill straightens his posture and shoots a gaze back to the parking lot and then centers his gaze back on me. "I'll be in touch after I have my lawyers draw up all the papers we need. Really good seeing you both."

"You too, Bill," I say.

He nods at each of us, and we smile until he turns and walks away. I turn toward my wife, extending my hand for her. "Hey, I know you're anxious to get back to Piper, but what do you say we take a quick walk around the park? We haven't really had much time to ourselves, and it will be nice to walk around for old times' sake."

"I love that idea." She laces her fingers through mine, and we step onto the winding paved path. She leans into me, shoulder brushing my arm as she lets out a dreamy sigh. "I forgot how pretty it is here."

I nod toward the frozen pond. "It is nice, but it's so much smaller than I remember. Actually, everything about Mapleton feels smaller. Or maybe I just got bigger." I chuckle at my own joke. We stroll as the sun peeks from behind a single cloud, like it's coming out just for us to enjoy our walk. When we get near the rink, she tugs at my arm, and points toward a tree near the edge. "Tell me that tree means something to you."

I huff out laughter before she finishes the question. "I remember you didn't have a coat on. You never wore a coat back then because you were Miss Tough."

"Details." She shakes her head, aiming a brilliantly flirty smile at me.

"And you were out here in heels," I add. "In February. On ice."

She looks like she's about to laugh but pauses before going on in a more thoughtful tone, "I always wore heels. I didn't see it then, but that might have been part of my act. My needing to be strong and look like everything is put together." She shakes her head as she takes an effortless step forward in her laced-up orthotics. "And I have the veins to prove it. I'm glad those days are over."

I look back toward the tree, and the years peel away.

I remember my hands had been shaking worse than the cold deserved. Lacey and I had only been dating about six months. I'd already moved away to play in the NHL, and our time together was limited. A whirlwind of late-night drives, long talks on the phone back when there were long-distance charges applied, and rare dates with kisses that made it impossible to think straight. I knew I couldn't live without her. I had a lot of doubts because she had dated Bill for years. He'd proposed, and she said no. I was over the long-distance thing and back in town for Valentine's Day. She looked so pretty, even wearing a pink shirt for the holiday. I came to this park to play hockey on the ice rink with some of my old teammates. Lacey stood there watching me. Just having her near me made my chest finally relax. I knew I needed her nearness forever...

It didn't make sense.

Even my mom said it was reckless. She adored Lacey, but she thought I should focus on hockey before getting married.

But I'd known from the first moment I held her at prom, I'd never get her out of my head. Once she made her way into my heart, the deal was sealed forever.

"Our first Valentine's Day," I say quietly. "I had to leave the next day, and I was terrified to lose you."

Her thumb brushes over my knuckles. "You said you didn't want to leave without me."

"It's funny, before you I said I'd never get married," I murmur. "But I knew I would love you forever. I didn't need to waste time pretending my feelings were less than that."

Her expression softens into something that still, after all these years, hits me square in the chest. "It's been a beautiful life. Hasn't it?" she whispers.

"Yeah," I say. "I'd say I got lucky. I got everything and more than I dreamed of."

Our gazes connect with the same thing on our minds, and we lean in for a kiss. The kiss is slow and deep in the way only years can mold. And just like that, the world around us fades.

To just her.

Acknowledgements

I always start these pages with a bit of an apology because I'm terrible at them. Half the time I avoid writing acknowledgments altogether because I *know* I'm going to forget someone important, and that stresses me out.

The truth is, there is absolutely no way I could write these books without this incredible book community. And there's also no way I could possibly name every single person who has supported me along the way.

So if you've ever shared one of my books, left a review, sent me a message, or even pointed out a typo with a screenshot, please know that it all means more to me than I can properly put into words. It feels like a bit of a copout to say "you know who you are," but I hope you do because you are so appreciated.

That said, I do have to try and name a few people.

To my family—thank you for putting up with me always being on my laptop, always "just finishing one more thing," and always living a little bit in my fictional worlds.

To my incredible editing team—thank you for your patience, your sharp eyes, and for never (publicly) judging the truly impressive number of typos I can stuff into a book.

To my ARC readers and Bookstagrammers—you are the heartbeat of this community. I'm endlessly grateful for the time and love you pour into supporting clean romance.

To Kerry Evelyn—my fellow hockey author and dear friend—thank you for cheering me on through this entire hockey journey. Having you in my corner has meant more than you know.

And most importantly, thank you to God.

I used to joke that I stumbled into hockey romance by accident after winning a free cover. But now, eight hockey romcom books in with many more stories on the way, I know it was never an accident. He was guiding me toward something I love.

I hope you enjoyed this story. It's a little different from my usual romcoms as it's more emotional than I typically go. (Don't worry, I still prefer laughter. Life is too short not to.)

God bless you all, and happy reading! JP

Also by J.P. Sterling

<u>Sweet Hockey RomCom (All Standalones)</u>

The Pucker-Up Pact

Shot Through the Heart

All I Need is my Glove

Till Sudden Death Do Us Part

<u>Sweet Hockey RomCom Adjacent (Standalone)</u>

Driving Miss Crazy

<u>Rivalry Rewritten (Duet)</u>

An Icicle Made for Two

Some Guys Get All the Pucks

<u>Timeless Christmas Tails (All Standalone)</u>

Have Yourself a Legendary Christmas

<u>Christmas Shenanigans (All Standalone)</u>

Mingle All the Way

Tis the Season to Get Married

Let's Not and Sleigh We Did

Hark! The Hot Santa Sings

<u>The Coffee Loft Series (All Standalones)</u>

Pardon My French Press

No More Mr. Chia Guy

Truely, Madly, Steeply Brew

<u>A Modern Fairy Tale Series (All Standalones)</u>

Royally Rugged

<u>Bosses and Billionaires Series (All Standalones)</u>

Maid for my Billionaire Boss

Knock! Knock! It's Your Enemy Boss

Kissed by My Billionaire Boss

Marooned with My Celebrity Boss

<u>A Heart that Dances Series</u>

Dancing on Broken Ankles

The Stars We See

A Heart that Dances

A Heart that Loves

<u>Water and Stone Duet</u>

Ruby in the Water

Lily in the Stone

About J.P. Sterling

J.P. Sterling grew up watching old reruns of Lucille Ball and Mary Tyler Moore and fell in love with wholesome entertainment and slapstick comedy. She loves leaning into the over-the-top humor and full circle moments, especially if it means the underdog gets to shine.

Aside from writing, she's also a wife, homeschooling mom, a holistic dietitian, a former college professor, and lover of all-things dark chocolate.

*No swears. Just kisses. No Blasphemies. *

Let's get social!

Hey, you amazing reader! You are invited to join my private reader group for all-things clean books and friends. Enter the group here: https://www.facebook.com/groups/15008507 64081965

Other places to follow me:

Instagram: https://www.instagram.com/stories/authorjp sterling/

Facebook: https://www.facebook.com/jpsterlingauthor/

Amazon: https://www.amazon.com/stores/author/B01 N9TJXJN/about